The Magician

The Magician

TIMOTHY GRAY

iUniverse, Inc.
New York   Bloomington

The Magician

iUniverse books may be ordered through booksellers or by contacting:

iUniverse
1663 Liberty Drive
Bloomington, IN 47403
www.iuniverse.com
1-800-Authors (1-800-288-4677)

ISBN: 978-1-4502-2793-3 (pbk)
ISBN: 978-1-4502-2794-0 (ebk)

Printed in the United States of America

iUniverse rev. date: 4/29/2010

In memory of Phyllis Gray and Kris Drew;
gone but not forgotten.

What happens in Vegas, stays in Vegas.

CHAPTER 1

"WHERE AM I?"

The words stuck in her throat.

"Hush, little sparrow," one of her captors said in a Southern-Cajun twang.

She tried to reach out to steady herself but remembered her hands were bound.

"But—" she started but left the word hanging. Her voice sounded alien in her ears, as if it belonged to somebody else. Where the hell was she? Was this freak show for real? One minute, she had been breathing in the sultry night air of the French Quarter on a beautiful Friday evening, and the next, she was being gift-wrapped in duct tape in the back of a windowless cargo van with shag carpet, which had a stereo loud enough to shake the Superdome and a musty funk that smelled like cat-pee soup inside. Since then, she'd been floating in and out of consciousness.

Now, after being dragged down a short flight of stairs, she was once again trying to find her bearings. The jokers with their paws all over her had finally removed the duct tape from her mouth, telling her no one could hear her scream. But she was still blind behind a thick layer of duct tape, and her wrists were still bound in front of her.

She repeated the question, this time framing it like a demand instead of a plea. "Where am I?"

"Don't make me repeat myself, small thing," the same voice said.

He was claustrophobically close, without even a trace of reverb to dampen his baritone voice. Wherever they were, they were in a sonically dead room, with a low ceiling, she guessed, and something soft and squishy beneath her feet. More shag carpet? God, what was wrong with these people? At least they could have taken her someplace that didn't violate health codes.

She felt the walls closing in again.

"Oh no you don't, butterfly," the man with the deep voice said and shook her lightly. "No more slipping into ethereal bliss. We need you awake now, honey pot. Stick with me. I'll see you through to the end. I'm the alpha and the omega, baby girl, the beginning and the end. Logos turned flesh. The darkness at the beginning of the tunnel. Do you have eyes to see? A mouth with which to taste? Ears to hear with? You know me, *mon amie*. I've come for you."

A chill traced her spine from top to bottom. Was this creep quoting the New Testament or a cheesy paperback with half-dressed lovers on the cover?

She felt his rough hands close around hers, which were still bound. Her fingers, tingling and clumsy, felt tiny in his leathery grip. He was furnace-hot.

"Please," she begged, "let me at least see you." She thought about all the rotten things she had done and promised God she would be a better person and give to charity if He spared her life. She thought about her dad and her poor dead mother and wished she was at home. Why had she ever left home? That was so stupid. She wanted to see her kitty, Spooky, and her ex-boyfriend, Rob. She wanted him to bust in the door and get her out of there and into the light. But Rob was living in Michigan now, married to her ex-best friend Trish. They weren't likely to form a search party anytime soon."

"Sorry, sweet *Yemanja*," he said and coughed out a filmy laugh. "Darkness is my gift to you. From whence we came, we all must return. I am the mighty wave, the undertow that pulls you down. The howling wind. The dust to dust. The sorcerer and the shroud. The darkness inside blackness. The tiger-tiger burning brightly. I've come for you."

"I know. I know," she said, her desperation creeping toward annoyance. "You've come for me. But why? Why me?" She was stalling now. "You don't even know me! You don't know my name. You don't know my father. You don't even know my cat!"

She felt his hands migrate to her shoulders, and suddenly, she was falling backward, the recipient of an unceremonious push. Someone caught her then.

"You ready, boy?" the man who caught her asked.

Her other captor's voice, until now delivered in a steady baritone cadence, squeaked. "Who you calling 'boy'?"

"Whatever, man. Let's get shiggy with this voodoo shit already. I wanna get back to catch the game on ESPN."

"It's not voodoo, you fool. It's *vodun*. Voodoo is something they sell to mindless tourists shopping for keepsakes in the French Quarter. *Vodun* is my sacred religion. And I am your *houngan*. I am your—"

"Bullshit," the man holding her said. "Last week, you was a Mayan priest. Now you're a freakin' witch doctor. Who you gonna be next? Chaka Khan?"

"Cut it!" a third voice screamed, spraying her face with spittle. "Get on with the ritual!" He was obviously talking to her as much as he was to the rest of them, and she knew at once that if the others didn't find the nerve, he would be the one to. The man with the deep voice liked to talk, and the man holding her liked to joke. But this one—this one was a different animal. He was cold to the core.

"Do you bring Death to our little mouse-girl?" the deep-voiced one asked. "Are you the Bringer?"

The Bringer's face was inches from hers. She could smell onions every time he opened his mouth. "What's your name?" he breathed.

"Jenny," she said, trying to sound brave. "Jenny Cross."

"Jenny," he said without a trace of emotion. "You're ready to piss yourself." He took a step back. "Get on with the ceremony."

"Do not fret, *mon amie*," the deep-voiced one whispered loud enough for everyone in the room to hear. "With the Bringer, you will feel no pain, just eternity, sweet and true."

"There he goes again," the man holding her said.

He pushed her forward and then let go, and she staggered to a standstill, suddenly feeling naked in the silence. No one spoke. No one touched her.

Finally, the Bringer stepped forward again. She knew him by the onions on his breath. She suspected he was circling her now.

"Do it to it," she heard the man who had been holding her say.

She heard a faint spinning sound and then flinched instinctively when a stereo began thumping rap music, the bass deep enough to make her heart palpitate. She thought she heard a siren, but the sound disappeared and morphed into a strangely seductive pulsing. She struggled against the duct tape wrapped tightly around her wrists but succeeded only in feeling utterly weak. She was surrounded by suffocating darkness.

Somewhere between here and the French Quarter, where she had nearly been torn from her shoes, lurked the story of her abduction. She tried to piece it together: the hurried steps behind her, the callused hand over her mouth, the other hands—it had felt like dozens of them—pulling her sharply into the van. She had been shocked by the sheer violence of it all, and her mind still refused to believe something so audacious could have happened to her. This couldn't be real. She couldn't be locked with a bunch of nonsense-talking monsters in a musty basement. *That was it!* She was in a basement. But where? Nobody had basements in New Orleans. At least nobody with any sense.

Someone turned the music down, and she heard the deep-voiced man reading aloud. "We come here to make manifest darkness," he said above the synthetic bass and drums, "to make an offering to the one pure light so that we might satisfy its hunger." His voice changed as he looked up from whatever he was reading. "Bring her to the altar."

She felt a pair of hands push into her back, and she was forced forward and then made to kneel.

"Sacrificial One," the deep-voiced one continued, addressing her now, "your time here was short but not spent in vain. Your role is a holy one. You feed the future. You feed the Full One. The Bringer has come to take you away."

She wanted to scream out, but no words came. Her heart beat so loudly that she could no longer hear the music, just the rhythmic pounding in her ears. Each thump felt like it had come for her, like it would be her last. *No!* a voice screamed inside her. *This can't be it!*

She finally found the nerve to speak. "Listen, you … you've got the wrong person. I'm not you're girl. I'm a recovering Catholic, for Christ's sake!"

She felt her face flush. Ever since her teen years, she had always made it a habit to laugh when she should have been crying, to crack a joke in the face of danger. But she'd never been here before, never laughed at death before. This wasn't real.

"Frail thing," the deep-voiced one said, "you're perfect!"

"Frail?" she protested. "I'd bust your nuts if it was a fair fight."

"Maybe in another lifetime," the man mused. "But you're not here for us. You're here to feed the Full One."

"You can't be serious," she scoffed. She'd barely uttered the words when she felt the sting of his hand against her cheek. She reeled from the blow.

"Silence, foolish girl!" Her captor's voice trailed away as he turned to say something to the others.

Then she felt the Bringer's breath on her face.

"Your time has come," the deep-voiced one said from somewhere nearby.

Someone's hands pried open her lips, and she found herself choking on room-temperature tap water.

Oh God, she thought. *This is it!*

"Say your prayers, girl," the Bringer whispered.

Before she could respond, she heard three loud pops, and she was sprayed in warm stickiness as the Bringer—or at least most of him—fell against her knees.

"Freeze!" someone hollered. "This is the police!"

There was a brief moment of eerie silence, where nothing could be heard but the faint pulse of the music in the background, and then the room erupted in chaos.

"You done it backward, cop man!" the deep-voiced man screamed. "You all funky backward! What you gone and done? You s'pposed to warn us '*fore* you shoot, fool! Hey! Let go of me!"

She could hear her captors being hustled to the ground and several people yelling orders. The acrid smell of gunpowder burned her nostrils.

Suddenly, she felt someone else's hands—rough but kind—prying the duct tape from her wrists and now her eyes.

"Ouch!" she squealed as the tape was wrestled free from her hair.

She shielded her eyes from the light pouring down from a naked ceiling bulb that dangled only a few inches above her. Finally, she squinted up to see a plainclothes detective staring down at her. A small town girl from Ponchatoula, she knew enough about New Orleans to know the city's police had a reputation for brutality, corruption, and even murder. But this one was different. He was a little rough around the edges, true, with his sandy brown hair going every which way and his eyebrows looking like an unmade bed above his steel-blue eyes, but he was different.

"You okay?" he asked.

She watched his gaze travel from her eyes to her blood-covered blouse.

"I think so?" she said, her voice trailing up, as if she'd just asked a question.

"Good shootin', Rambo," a uniformed officer said as he and another policeman ushered out two of her would-be executioners.

She guessed the one dressed in a robe was the one who'd done all the talking. The other, a skinny gangbanger wearing expensive high-tops and baggy jeans, would, alas, be missing the big game on ESPN.

She glanced down at the Bringer, now dead as a doornail and still gripping something sharp and shiny, and then back up at the detective, who was smiling a crooked smile.

"You saved my life," she said and blushed. "With shooting like that, I'm guessing you're from Texas, right?"

"Oh, hell no," he said. "Detective O'Meara. John O'Meara. I'm from the Bronx, not Houston."

"Thank God," she said.

~~~

Detective O'Meara studied the girl leaning against his patrol car, arms folded, teeth chattering. It was another steamy night in what was left of the Lower Ninth, but she was freezing.

"Here," he said and handed her a blanket from his trunk. "I'd give you my jacket, but I didn't wear one today."

"Thank you." She took it and wrapped herself in it, still shivering. "How'd you guys find me?"

"Dumb luck. Got a tip from a tacky voodoo shop in the French Quarter. Store owner overheard a couple of amateurs talking about sacrificing a girl. She saved the receipt and called us. We were able to trace the car registration but couldn't find a valid home address. Thought we'd hit a dead end, but a couple of officers doing a routine patrol out here spotted his car about an hour later." He nodded to the tricked-out Acura parked out front. "We thought we'd beaten them to the punch, but we were almost too late."

The girl shuddered. At about 5 feet 7 inches tall with long brunette hair, she looked like the proverbial girl next door, although the detective thought he spied something mischievous in her brown eyes. He guessed her to be in her early twenties—twenty-six at the most—a lot younger than him. Despite her ordeal, she was holding it together quite well. She was a survivor, although clearly lost. He watched as she glanced across the street at the boarded-up houses and then at the sidewalk, where weeds were growing knee-high between the cracks in the cement.

"Where are we?"

"The Lower Nine, part of my beat. I'm with the Fifth District."

"Lower Nine? As in the Lower Ninth Ward?"

"You got it."

"I thought there was nothing left after Katrina."

"Not much—that's for sure. We've stepped up our patrols 'cause the crack dealers are moving back in. They love these old boarded-up houses, especially the ones with basements."

"Basements? Who'd be stupid enough to—"

"They're grandfathered in. It's against building codes now, or if it isn't, it sure as hell should be. Basements below sea level tend to flood, even without the benefit of a Category Five hurricane." He removed a pen and a small spiral notepad from his shirt pocket and gathered his thoughts. "I know you've been through quite a bit, but I need to ask you a few questions."

The girl flashed a gorgeous smile. "Sure."

"Well, for starters, what's your name?"

"Jenny Cross."

"Where you from, Jenny?"

"Ponchatoula," she said and then stopped herself. "At least that's where I was from until last week. I got an apartment near the French Quarter. Got a job waitressing. It's not what I want to do the rest of my life, mind you, but I had to get out."

"Oh?" Detective O'Meara briefly considered prying but decided to keep to the subject at hand. "Can you tell me what happened?"

"I was walking home from work, just enjoying the beautiful evening. It was only my second day on the job. Next thing I know, these guys grab me and stuff me into their van. The one you shot—he was creepy. I think the other two may have been all bark, but he definitely bit. He wanted to kill me."

"Yeah, I had that same thought when we got here and saw him reach for his switchblade."

She laughed at his lame joke, and the detective got a funny feeling in his gut. Was she flirting with him? He tried to stay focused on his job. "I know everything went pretty fast back there, but did you recognize any of the suspects, including the, uh, dead one?"

"Recognize them?"

"Yeah, have you seen them before?"

"If I had, I wouldn't remember it. Like I said, I've only been here a week. Everything and everybody is new to me." She raised an eyebrow. "Including you."

Again with the flirting, he thought. *That's obvious, right? She's flirting, right?*

"Well," he stammered, "I guess that's all I need for now. Are you okay? You look okay. I mean, you look *great*, other

than, you know, that guy's blood all over your … front."
Where was a two-by-four when he needed one? He felt like
delivering a self-inflicted wound or at least stuffing his foot
into his mouth. Then again, maybe he already had.

She laughed again, rolling her lovely brown eyes. "I'm fine.
Can you take me home?"

CHAPTER 2

DETECTIVE JOHN O'MEARA rolled out of bed Saturday morning and stretched. His lower back was sorer than usual, and he felt a sensation foreign to him most mornings—hunger. He looked down at Jenny still resting peacefully in his bed. *So much for taking her home.*

She stirred softly beneath the sheets and then opened her eyes. "Hey."

"Hey, yourself. You sleep okay?"

She smiled broadly. "Uh-huh."

"You want some coffee?"

"Sure," she said and stretched under the covers, modestly covering just enough of herself.

The detective slipped on a pair of jeans and a T-shirt and left for the kitchen, where he started brewing some coffee. This was usually about the time he started panicking, but he felt strangely calm, as if this was exactly the way things were supposed to go: save attractive girl from low-rent voodoo hacks, trade stories over drinks, and end up back at his place for a movie and a friendly shag. He fought the urge to feel guilty for taking advantage of someone fifteen years his junior and in such a vulnerable state.

"Don't worry," Jenny then said. "I'm a big girl."

He looked up to see Jenny wearing a button-up shirt from his closet—and most likely nothing else.

"I—"

"I know that look," she said, cutting him off. She took hold of the belt loops on both sides of his jeans. "You're wondering how much trouble you've just gotten yourself into."

John smiled in disbelief. This kid was something else. "How old are you, anyway?"

She kissed him gently on the cheek and then batted her eyelashes coyly. "You first."

"All right. Thirty-eight," he lied. He was actually forty-four, but what the hell.

She took a step back. "Really?" she asked, looking genuinely surprised. "I would have guessed thirty-one, tops."

"Flattery will get you nowhere."

"I'm not flattering you. You look great for someone … your age. You must work out."

"Among other things," he said, suddenly feeling self-conscious. When he looked in the mirror these days, he saw less hair on his forehead and more everywhere else. But who was he to destroy her illusions? He tried to redirect the conversation. "Still waiting for your answer."

"Twenty-five," she said matter-of-factly and then poured herself a cup of coffee now that the coffeemaker had bubbled to a stop.

"Whew," he said. "At least you're not young enough to be my daughter."

"Hey," she protested, "you said last night you don't have any kids or ex-wives. No 'baggage,' remember?"

"And that's still the truth," he said. "I was speaking figuratively just now. We do that in the big city."

She set her coffee mug on the counter next to her and took his hands in hers. "We need to get something straight, officer."

"Detective."

"Whatever." She shot him an ornery glance and continued. "The point is, *detective*, you may have rescued me last night, and you may be a big city boy and older than me and all that, but I'm not some helpless country bumpkin, okay? I can take care of myself. I'm here because I want to be, not because you took advantage of me or because I'm in shock or something." Her voice seemed to trail off when she finished.

He spotted a vulnerable look in her eyes and knew she was speaking wishfully. "Got it," he said. "No more teasing. And no more worrying. I promise not to chew my arm off the next time we end up in bed."

She pulled back playfully. "Next time?"

"Right," he said. "You're in charge." He tried to change the subject. "So tell me more about Ponchatoula. I've only been there a few times. What's there besides a whole bunch of strawberries?"

"Oh, it's just like any little tourist town."

"How so?"

"You know," she said with a shrug of her shoulders, "charming on the surface but hollow underneath. There's the strawberry festival and some art galleries and some old stuff to look at like the old train depot, but when you get right down to it, a small town's a small town. Everybody knows everybody, and everybody's business is everybody's business. The place changes at glacial speed. Pretty much everybody my age eventually wants out." She walked to the sliding glass door that led to the balcony. "Not much of a view," she said, staring out at the backside of another apartment building.

"That's Marigny, baby," he said unapologetically. "It's a blue-collar neighborhood. Or at least it used to be. Now everyone's talking about gentrification." He opened the door and led her out onto the second-story balcony. "Look down there," he said and pointed to a row of glossy-leaved southern Magnolias, each of them not much more than five or six feet tall. "Who says this isn't Shangri-La? A couple years and I'll be staring at a forest."

She laughed, showing off her gorgeous smile once again. "So tell me about your job. You always shoot first and ask questions later?"

"I try not to ask questions at all," he said and let a smirk emerge. "What do you wanna know?"

"I don't know," she said. "Like, how often do you bust in on a gang of witch doctors?"

He chuckled and shook his head. "More often than you'd think. The guys at the station say I have a sick sense."

"A *sixth* sense?"

"No. *Sick*. A *sick* sense. As in, *I don't feel well*. If there's a body parts smuggling ring out there or a grave robber or a crack addict channeling Marie Laveau's ghost, I'll find 'em. You wouldn't believe half the stuff I've seen." He stopped himself short. "I don't believe half of it myself."

"Marie Laveau?"

"You know, the lady who brought voodoo to New Orleans in the eighteen hundreds. People still leave flowers at her tomb."

"Oh, her. Why do you think voodoo is so popular here?"

"Good question. I know Katrina left people looking for answers—you know, 'Why us?' and all that. But it's always been popular here, and not just with the tourists."

"Okay. So what's behind all the strange things you've seen?"

Damn, she was inquisitive. And awfully attractive. It was hard to refuse her anything. He thought of their encounter last night. The same deep brown eyes that were staring at him now were the ones responsible for landing them in bed together.

"Tough to say," he finally answered and led her back inside past the sliding glass door. "Maybe all the above-ground crypts. I don't know."

She cocked her head in disbelief. "Really? You don't strike me as the type to believe in ghosts."

"I don't," he said. "Just throwing it out there. I have no idea what makes this city's underworld tick. All I know is I seem to be the first on the scene whenever a lovely maiden's about to be sacrificed."

"Oh," she said mischievously. "So I'm not the first?"

"Of course not," he said, deciding to play along. "You're merely the latest in a long line of stunningly attractive young women from Ponchatoula to fall for this broken-down cop."

"You're not broken down," she said, suddenly sounding earnest. There was that look in her eyes again. She sure as hell had it all: charm, intelligence, and passion.

"So tell me more about why you left what I assume was a steady job in Ponchatoula for a waitressing gig in New Orleans," he said.

A handful of wrinkles fanned out across her forehead as she thought the question over. "You want the short version or the long one?"

"I want the truth," he joked. "You can spill it to me now. Or we can go downtown, and you can try your luck with the lie detector at the station."

She laughed. "Fine. Long story. But you better start cooking something. I'm starved."

"Me too," he said, remembering his grumbling stomach. "You like omelets?"

"Sure. But do you mind sifting out the yolks? I have my girlish figure to consider."

Girlish? More like hourglass. He hurriedly got to work separating several yolks from their shells. "So tell me the long story. What's in New Orleans for you?"

"Well, it's not so much what's here as it is what *isn't* back there."

"Go on."

"My dad runs an antique shop in Ponchatoula right across

from the old railroad depot. Has for years. He opened it with his dad before I was even born."

"What about your mom?"

"I'm getting there," she said with a pout. "My parents separated when I was eight. My mom went to live back in New York with her parents."

"New York City?"

"Uh-huh."

"Where?"

"Oh, they had a few different addresses. All of 'em in Manhattan. Anyway, I was supposed to follow her once she got settled in, but she got real sick—she was always sick with diabetes—and died. So I stayed with my dad. Dad's a good guy, but he and Mom were never right for each other. He's a conservative, old-school, hardcore Catholic. She was a free spirit, a bit of an artist, always playing the devil's advocate, always causing people to raise their eyebrows in our little town. At least that's what my dad says. I don't remember much of her anymore. It's been so long."

John loved the way her thick hair bounced when she talked. Her hands did a lot of the talking, too.

"But Dad says I'm the spitting image of her, and I think I have the same habits of asking questions and causing trouble that she did. Dad taught me the business, and I did the books for him and all that, never went to college, yada yada. But I just couldn't see myself spending the rest of my life in Ponchatoula, ending up like all the other unhappy spinsters there. And the whole Catholic thing." She stopped then and thought for a moment before she asked, "Are you religious?"

"Not so anyone would notice."

"Okay, good. I mean, it would be fine if you were. I just didn't want to offend you or anything. Anyway, I eventually stopped going to Mass, started traveling whenever I got the chance, started reading a lot, basically driving my dad nuts. I finally told him I had to get out. He was crushed. I think he truly thought I'd spend the rest of my life running the antique shop. And moving to New Orleans of all places! I think he'd disown me if he didn't love me so much."

"So you didn't leave on a bitter note?"

"No, not at all. He understands. I'm my mother's daughter."

Jenny spoke more about growing up in Ponchatoula, reviving lost fragments from her childhood and her memory of her mother, and then the two sat down to a breakfast of ham-and-cheese omelets, with toast, orange juice, and more black coffee.

When they had finished, John got up to shower. Jenny's stories were entertaining at moments, poignant at others, but they did nothing to remove what had been gnawing at him for several days now. Like Jenny, he had lost someone special in his family.

Three special people, in fact. First came his younger sister Madeline, who had died of leukemia at the tender age of six. Next came both of his parents, who had been killed in a car crash one fateful night while he was in high school. He had lived the rest of his youth with his aunt and uncle in a nearby neighborhood in the Bronx, and he had spent most of those years protecting his youngest sister, Payton, a sweet-natured girl born three years to the day after Madeline's death. Her perennial champion and protector, John felt inexplicably linked to her, the last surviving member of his immediate family, and to this day, he regularly checked in on her to make sure she was okay. A couple days earlier, he had been unable to reach her. He was worried that—

The shower door opened, and there stood Jenny, sans John's dress shirt, which had been dropped unceremoniously on the floor. As he had suspected, she had been wearing only her birthday suit beneath it.

"Got room for one more?"

"Sure, as long as you don't mind sharing the soap."

"I don't mind."

She took the soap from him and closed the shower door behind her, a mischievous look in her eyes.

"Look, Jenny," John said, trying to focus on what he'd just been turning around in his mind, "I need to run some errands, and then I'm flying out of town for the weekend."

She pursed her lips. "Oh," she said, clearly trying to sound upbeat. "If you need me to—"

"No, take your time. You can let yourself out when you're ready to go home." As he said the word, he realized *home* was one thing the girl from Ponchatoula didn't have at the moment. Last night's seduction had followed at least partially from one simple fact: she was afraid to go back to her studio apartment. "On second thought, make yourself at home. I'll leave my cell number by the phone in case you need to get a hold of me while I'm gone."

"No, no," Jenny said, obviously forcing a smile. "You didn't sign on for a roommate last night." The smile on her face faded, and she stepped closer until their bodies were touching. "So where are you going?"

"Las Vegas."

She lifted an eyebrow. "Gambling problem?"

"I wish." He was torn between honoring the thoughts weighing on his mind and succumbing to the pleasure in his immediate future. "A family matter."

"You know all about mine," Jenny said. She was talking barely above a whisper now, her lips only inches from his. "I don't know anything about yours."

"I'll tell you sometime," he said, no longer able to think straight.

"Promise?"

"I promise."

Jenny's eyebrows met as a worried expression crossed her face. "Did I mention I get premonitions?"

"No."

"I just got an awful feeling about Vegas," she whispered, "like maybe this weekend is just the start of something big. And bad."

"Don't worry," he said. Her skin against his made everything else disappear. "I'll be fine."

Chapter 3

Jokers, Sadie thought. *Know-nothings.*

She eyed the two businessmen drooling at the sight of her and tried not to laugh. Both white, both middle-aged, both shaped like overripe pears—they were her most loyal customers. Las Vegas swarmed with them. They would return again and again and again some more.

But sometimes, she couldn't stomach the condescension. Sometimes, even knowing she would have the last laugh wasn't enough. The mere fact that she had to play nice before she could play her way was enough to ruin her fun. She wasn't one of them, didn't walk in their world. But knowing they saw themselves as her economic and cultural masters made her grind her teeth. *If they only knew.*

"Hey, honey," the blotchier of the two said. "Let me buy you a drink."

"No thanks," she said. "You can't afford what I drink."

The two men jerked their heads back in unison as they laughed at her effrontery.

"She's a spunky one, ain't she?" the other said as soon as he recovered himself.

"I'll say," the blotchy one drawled. "Sugar, how come I

don't see you up there onstage? You got something to hide under that skimpy little outfit?"

"Don't look like it to me," the other one said. "She's bustin' out at the seams."

"Gentleman," she said, "you'll have to excuse me. There's someone else who needs my services."

She turned her back on the stuffed shirts and let her ears burn as they unloosed a blue streak in disbelief. On them, she smelled only drunk lust. Their overindulged libidos didn't boast the bravado of youth but the dysfunction of middle age.

She was after a different scent—the smell of fear—and she followed it, her long legs chewing up the tiles beneath her, until she arrived at a table for one, its owner hunched against the back wall.

My sweet loser, she thought. *Won't you be mine?*

"Hey," she cooed just loud enough to be heard above the throbbing house music that blared from the speaker hanging above him, "you alone?"

He nodded self-consciously, still hiding behind the table.

She stepped closer, stooping just enough to give him a tantalizing view of the gorgeous, God-given C-cups lurking beneath her black satin negligee. "You lonely?"

Before he could answer, she closed what little space remained between them and waited as his nostrils filled with her sweet-scented perfume.

She was sure he was a traveling salesman. She knew the type. As opposed to the jokers back at the bar, he was embarrassed to be here. He traveled alone. Slept and ate economically. The modest gold band on his left ring finger said he was married. With two kids, no doubt. One of each. He probably loved his wife or at least worried about disgracing her. But he had a fire inside him that his wife had long since stopped feeding. The burning sensation was strong enough to make him forget everything that mattered. Domesticity was the enemy of passion. A kept man was a dead man.

Sadie pressed her lips gently against his ear. "Why don't you come with me, darling? I'll dance just for you."

She took his left hand, the one with the wedding ring, and led him across the room, past the bar, past the disbelieving stuffed shirts, past the other girls dressed like medieval vixens, and into a back room.

She nodded to the burly bouncer guarding one of several doors, and he nodded in return without making eye contact. She knew he, like all the other male employees, wanted her as much as the patrons, because she was different—better—than the other girls at the club. Like every gentlemen's club on the Strip, this one was stocked with beauties. Brunettes, blondes, redheads. White, black, brown. Petite, Amazonian, deliciously plump. But none of them had what she had.

As she closed the door behind her guest, she could almost hear the blood rushing to his cheeks. The room was tiny and claustrophobically warm. A plush velvet loveseat with blood-red fabric and gold-painted woodwork was the room's sole furnishing. A wall-mounted lamp, dimly lit, cast shadows on the carpeted floor.

She fingered a strand of her chin-length, blue-black bob and took in the lonely, small man in front of her. "Do you want me?" she whispered.

He gulped the words. "I do."

"Do you *need* me?"

He nodded yes.

She dropped her sheer robe to the floor and then toyed with the spaghetti straps at her shoulders. All she could feel was hunger—wild and insatiable. The man in front of her was not perfect by any means, but he at least had humility and a conscience that made him tremble with regret. He had made the decision to do whatever it was they were about to do. He was ready to give himself to her.

She felt her face flush with red heat and was soon overcome with a familiar sensation, one of utter release and abandon. Would he go willingly? Or would she have to fight for what belonged to her?

Pain, torturous yet exquisite, enveloped her body, and she suddenly felt like a snake shedding its old skin. The moment had arrived. She was being born again.

His eyes widened at the sight of her, and she heard his heart in her ears, a jackhammer on a pogo stick. Would he run? Sink to the floor? She had picked him, because he had looked like the type to go quietly. Tonight, unlike some nights, she was too tired to work for her dinner.

He backed away feebly—too slow, too unsure. Perhaps he didn't believe his eyes. His mouth, opening wider by the second, knew no words. He was frozen in fear. She took his hips in her hands, jerked him around, and slammed him hard enough against the wall to crack the plaster.

Oops, she thought. *Too rough.*

She brought her mouth to his neck and whispered, "To your health."

~~~

John O'Meara almost dropped his drink when he heard a woman shriek, "There it is! The Strip!" The woman was sitting in the window seat ahead of him and tugging at her husband's arm.

As his plane descended toward Las Vegas Boulevard South, John glanced out the window at a familiar site, namely the gleaming Strip, most of which was south of Las Vegas proper. Tonight's redeye flight was, for him at least, old hat. He'd been here dozens of times for weekend bachelor parties, other long descents into hedonism, and the odd convention.

But the sight of Vegas lighting up the night sky never failed to energize him, even from several thousand feet up. The plush hotels, the neon replicas of monuments like the Eiffel Tower, the long stream of headlights wading through the

Strip—Vegas turned night into day, excess into civic pride, and vice into virtue (or at least something so common it could be bandied about in broad daylight without remorse). The desert city's Day-Glo façade and unapologetic opulence stood in stark contrast to John's hometown and its decaying outer districts like the Lower Ninth, still in ruins from Hurricane Katrina, still waiting on relief that would never come.

In contrast to shell-shocked New Orleans, which was mired in inaction and apathy, Vegas looked like the city of hope, a place where a jackpot was always just around the corner. Anything could happen here. No dream was too outlandish or too gauche. If New Orleans had been left to rot, Las Vegas had been enjoying an eternal bloom as the capital of overindulgence, where money was thrown around promiscuously and the night sky made daylight look dull.

So what the hell was Payton doing here? Why had his sister, always so levelheaded, always so responsible, fallen off the map? She had always called him at least once a week, sometimes more. So why hadn't he heard from her in two weeks? As a schoolteacher back in the Bronx where they had grown up, she had always been the more mature of the two, even if she was nine years his junior. Yes, she had a good excuse for going off the deep end. Her loser husband had run off with his secretary—enough said. And yes, she'd never really explored the world outside of the Bronx. She wasn't necessarily too young to try something new. But Vegas?

With her teaching career on hold, thanks to a year-long sabbatical, Payton had found an apartment in Vegas and was shopping herself to casinos, modeling agencies, movie producers, anybody in the entertainment world who would have her. At twenty-nine, she was older by a decade than most women taking their first crack at stardom. But she had talent—a lovely singing voice, which she had discovered while she had done theater in college—and a beautiful smile. More than that, she had brains and a personality, too. Then why hadn't she called him?

John grinned to himself as he imagined her chatting up a booking agent or a photographer. She wasn't the typical vacuous would-be star. She had an intellect and real-life experiences. The gatekeepers would probably want to hire her just to have someone of her caliber working for them.

But why Vegas? Shouldn't she have gone to Hollywood or Chicago or stayed in New York? As John turned the problem over in his head, it dawned on him that his misgivings had mostly to do with the fact that his kid sister should have been thinking about settling down and having kids by now, not chucking her job and shooting the moon in Vegas.

His thoughts drifted to their childhood. He remembered the time Payton, about six years old, had come to him, sobbing, asking him to fix her dolly. The neighborhood bully had taken it and yanked off its hair. John had fixed her dolly, of course. It was just that kind of thing that had kept them close over the years. John had never told Payton, but he had also had a little "talk" with the bully. By God, no one was going to mess with his sister.

"Excuse me, sir. Your seatbelt?"

John looked up to see a bleached-blonde stewardess motioning to his unsecured seatbelt.

"Right," he said and clicked it firmly shut. Despite the runway at McCarran Airport coming into view, he had ignored the pilot's instructions while he pondered his sister's disappearance.

Disappearance. He wasn't quite sure he was ready to use the word. That was why he'd jumped on a plane—to rule out the unthinkable. Payton had moved to Vegas six weeks ago to "follow some leads," as she had put it. She had been feeding John regular updates until two weeks ago, when she had called to tell him she'd be away from her phone for a few days. No details. No information on where he could contact her in case of an emergency. Just a quick message on his voice mail. Since John had left the Bronx for New Orleans a decade and a half ago, he and his sister had never been out of touch for more than a week, much less two.

Where was she? He had always felt connected to his sister, almost telepathically so, although he knew the idea was ludicrous. But now, when he tried to imagine where his sister was or what she was doing, he drew a complete blank.

~~~

"Watch the road," Apollo grunted.

T-Bone gripped the steering wheel loosely with one hand while he fished a cigarette free from his shirt pocket. "Shut up," he said without looking at his passenger or the road ahead of him. He knew the road out of Vegas into no-man's-land like the back of his hand. Even at two in the morning, the lonely desert highway was scorching hot and boring.

"*You* shut up," Apollo said lazily.

"Jesus Christ." Why did Sadie always have to send him out here with Apollo? Why not one of the other bouncers? Anybody with half a brain. Apollo was nothing but muscle from his neck to his feet. Apollo must have been the stupidest white man who had ever lived. Stegosauruses were blessed with bigger cranial cavities. It was bad enough he had to clean up Sadie's VIP room every time she went on a binge. What was he? A frickin' janitor? At least everything in the room was varying shades of red. Otherwise the job would have been murder. As for these road trips to Bum-Fuck Egypt, he'd rather have spend them alone with the radio. Then maybe he'd get a chance to chill a while, without Apollo's constant nagging. The dude was like having a 300-pound wife.

"So who's the stiff in the trunk?" Apollo asked.

"Don't know. Don't care," T-Bone said, hoping to shut the conversation down in advance.

"You think he knew something?"

T-Bone exhaled a long, steady sigh. "No, I don't think he knew something. Just another midnight snack for Sadie."

"At least he's a he and not a she," Apollo said. "You know what I mean?"

Shit. There it was—the segue that led to another mindless rant from the muscle-bound brain donor that was Apollo. *You know what I mean?*

"I mean, it's like …" Apollo groped for the right word. "I don't mind burying some horny loser. Don't get me wrong. That shit's fun. But lately, we keep digging graves for beauties, and I can't stand putting 'em six feet under. I mean, what a waste, you know? I mean, that broad last week—she was grade-A meat, you know? She was like the Venus de Nilo, man. A work of art. Why'd Sadie have to go and drain her?"

"Milo."

"Huh?"

"It's Venus de *Milo*. Not Nilo."

"Oh."

T-Bone spied the cutoff and pulled onto the gravel road, dimming his headlights as he did. "If I was you," he said, "I'd avoid asking those types of questions."

"What type of questions is that?"

"The type that'll get you killed, dumb ass."

"Don't be calling me dumb ass!" Apollo said, his voice jiggling from the rough road. "I don't say nothing like that about you, do I?"

"Nope. That's because I'm not a dumb ass."

"You're lucky I don't bounce you through the windshield."

"I'd like to see you try it," T-Bone said. He was older and smaller than Apollo but no weaker. He could handle anyone. Anyone human, anyway.

He pulled the Caddy to a stop and killed the engine. "Let's get this shit done."

They went to work with their shovels, and the ground as

27

usual was rocky and unforgiving. Sadie insisted they do their digging here instead of somewhere closer to town, where wind and rain might conspire to reveal a blood-drained corpse.

"Shit," Apollo said, sweat dripping from his unibrow, "we need to hire us a backhoe."

"That's real discreet."

"At least we wouldn't be here all night trashing our backs."

T-Bone jammed his shovel into the growing pile of dirt and stood up straight. "I wish you'd stop complaining. Hell, I wish you'd stop talking."

"What you got against me?"

T-Bone stared at Apollo's features: the closely shorn head, the blue-black five o'clock shadow, and the olive-toned skin that looked sickly green in the pale moonlight. "Nothing, man. Keep digging."

"No, not till you tell me what gives."

"All right," T-Bone said. "You talk too much. You *whine* too much. You're always flapping your jaw."

"At least I don't eat people like the folks we work for."

"See, there you go. *Whining.* Here's the deal. If you wanna disappear somewhere, that's fine with me. I figure I'll have to do as much myself someday. That or I'll end up buried out here with the rest of Sadie's snack packs. But until then, there ain't no use complaining about it. It just makes it worse."

"Yeah," Apollo said thoughtfully. "Maybe you're right. Still, I hate to bury beautiful ladies."

"Well, focus on the present. The guy in the trunk ain't no damsel in distress. Just some traveling salesman about to become worm fodder. Maybe Sadie's turned over a new leaf. Maybe she's settled on loser dudes for the time being."

"I sure hope so," Apollo said, his eyes glowing white in the shadowy moonlight. "I'm tired of burying beauties."

CHAPTER 4

AFTER HE FLASHED his badge and tipped the apartment manager a twenty, Detective John O'Meara slipped the key into the lock and slipped inside, closing the door behind him. He paused to take stock of his sister's studio apartment. Nothing on the walls. No dishes stacked in the sink or junk mail piled on the kitchen counters. Painfully tidy. Everything white. Man, she was neat. Always had been, even as a kid. She had been the first one at the dinner table. The last one to finish off her Halloween candy. The only one to remember to say please and thank you—and really mean it. She had never made anyone feel guilty. Had never played the martyr. She was who she was, cheerfully and sometimes defiantly so. *It had to take work*, he thought, *to be so happy.*

At least she used to be happy. Now she was ... something else. Not exactly its mirror opposite but definitely restless. She was changing.

He squinted against the morning sunlight coming through the kitchen window. Where to look first? It felt a bit strange sneaking into Payton's apartment, but what choice did he have? She would want him—*expect* him—to come looking if she was in trouble.

He opened the refrigerator and found it mostly empty,

aside from a few condiments in the door and a six-pack of diet soda sitting on the top shelf. The thing even *smelled* clean. No surprise there. He shut the door and took a quick glance at the small kitchen. Payton loved to cook, but the usual telltale signs that she'd been busy in the kitchen—onions and cloves of garlic stacked side by side in a small bowl, tomatoes ripening in the window, cast-iron pans hanging above the stove—were conspicuously absent. Either she'd known ahead of time that she'd be gone for a while, or the girl had been going nonstop and was too busy to do her own cooking. Then again, she was always talking about how much she loved to cook for other people: her husband, her brother, and her friends.

John winced at the thought of his kid sister eating alone, her husband long gone. *The jackass.* Her husband, a perpetually stressed-out mortgage broker, had left her after he had entertained a two-year fling with his secretary. *Gee, how original.*

She'd only been in Vegas six weeks, the last half of which she had spent somewhere else, obviously, but he was surprised she'd done nothing to make the place feel like home. Was she focused on the task at hand? Suffering from short-timer's disease? Too busy to bother with nesting, another of her specialties?

She'd definitely found a sweet home base in Vegas. Her second-floor apartment overlooked a pool and courtyard lined with palm trees, and though hers was a studio apartment with no true bedroom, it felt plenty roomy and bright, thanks to tall ceilings and a southern exposure.

A quick check of the bathroom showed it, too, was barely broken in.

He returned to the main room and stepped down to the sunken living room and bedroom area, where the beige carpet was still crisscrossed with the trail left by a vacuum cleaner. The daybed had been stripped, and a tidy pile of sheets and blankets had been left at the foot of it. He let his gaze drift until it settled on a collection of newspapers and books stacked neatly on an end table.

Now he was getting somewhere. He sat down, tossed the books onto the bed, and sifted through the newspapers. The top page, dated just two days before his sister's last phone call, was open to the want ads, a handful of which had been circled. *Eureka!*

As he read through the handful of circled ads, he felt his jaw harden. Luxor, Caesar's Palace, Bellagio—it looked like every luxury hotel casino on the Strip was hiring. But the jobs available were service positions, not entertainment ones. Had Payton come all the way to Vegas just to serve cocktails to lubricated gamblers? Was she planning on taking the long road to success? Paying her dues? Going through the back door?

He decided to try to call her. Again. He had tried countless times over the past two weeks. As he tossed the newspapers aside, he flipped open his Motorola and punched Payton's number. At least, the one programmed as hers. But it rang and rang, not even going to voicemail. *Damn!* He closed his phone in disgust.

He sighed heavily. *She shouldn't be here*, he thought. *She should be back home teaching.*

~~~

With newspaper in hand, John took a taxi to the Strip. First stop: Bellagio. The place was like a mini Versailles, or so he imagined. He'd never actually been to the former court of Louis XIV. But every monument to excess—pools the size of small lakes, fountains moving enough water to irrigate most of rural Nevada, a palatial hotel blotting out the morning sun—was readily on display.

He made his way to the human resources department on the first floor, but predictably, given that it was a Sunday, the office was locked. He was about to turn around and return to the front lobby when he heard sneakers squeaking across the floor. He turned to see a young woman, barely out of college, buried beneath a box full of files and headed straight for him.

"Here. Let me help you," he said and assisted the girl, who had a blonde head of hair, golden skin, and an athletic build. She wore no makeup and was dressed in jogging shorts and a T-shirt.

"Thank you," she said and fumbled for her keys.

"Do you work here?"

"Just started Friday," she said and let herself in.

John followed with the box of files.

"Are you an assistant? An intern?"

She leveled a steely gaze at the detective. "I'm Jennifer Greenfield, head of Human Resources. And you are?"

"Sorry," John said and set the box down on the front desk. "I'm Detective John O'Meara with the New Orleans Police Department."

"Not looking for a job, I hope."

He laughed. Ms. Greenfield was young but no pushover. "Actually, I'm looking for my sister, who I believe has gone missing. I think she might have showed up here about three weeks ago looking for a job."

"Are you here on official police business?"

"I'm not on the clock, if that's what you mean. But I'm hoping you can help me."

"Okay," she said and motioned for him to follow her.

John picked up the box of files and followed the young woman to her back office, which was cluttered with more boxes, most of them unopened, and reams and reams of paperwork.

"Wow," he said as he took in the chaos. "You're jumping in with both feet." He removed a photo of Payton, all smiles, from his wallet and handed it over. "She's looking for a job in the entertainment industry."

"I see," Ms. Greenfield said. "We don't hire entertainers, just service personnel. Any entertainers are hired through outside booking agents." She studied the photo of Payton. "She has a nice smile."

"She does," John said impatiently. "You just got here, so you wouldn't recognize her. But perhaps someone on your staff—"

The young woman nodded, anticipating his request. "Right. I'll make a photocopy of her picture and keep it on my desk, along with your card."

"Great," John said and waited in her office as she copied off his sister's photo on the machine in the hallway.

As soon as she returned with the photo, he fired another question her way. "So tell me," he said, "I don't know the entertainment industry well. Why would someone hoping to break into the entertainment field go looking for a service job at a hotel casino?"

"Well," Ms. Greenfield said, "I think that's standard practice here just like in Los Angeles. Actors and musicians often try to land jobs where the action is. Then they use their position to hand out business cards or demos or whatever. It's a pretty decent strategy for someone trying to get their foot in the door."

John dropped his business card on her desk. "If you learn anything, give me a call."

"I'll do that," Ms. Greenfield said and showed him to the door.

~~~

Next up was Luxor Hotel and Casino, a mini city unto itself, with pools, spas, and an enormous casino, among other amenities, the latter of which was housed in a pyramid-shaped building that, like Bellagio, was big enough to blot out the sun.

Once again, the human resources department was closed for the weekend, but this time, John decided to try one of the lounges on the ground floor. It was early, and the joint was nearly empty, which meant he wouldn't have to fight to get the bartender's attention. The bartender, in fact, was alone and toweling off the counter. He looked like he'd been up all night.

"Hey," John said as he sidled up to the bar. "Rough night?"

"Par for the course," the bartender said without looking up. "Hate to break it to you, buddy, but we're closed."

"No worries. I'm not here for the booze." John set his sister's photo on the bar. "I'm looking for this woman."

The bartender took a quick glance at it and then resumed his cleaning. "You a cop?"

"Uh-huh."

"You talk funny. You from around here?"

"New Orleans."

"You sound more like you're from Brooklyn."

"The Bronx, actually."

The bartender took another look at Payton's photo, rubbing his sideburns. "Sorry, man, I see a lot of pretty girls, but I'm drawing a blank on this one."

"She would have come here looking for a job."

"Now *that* I'd remember. We don't have anyone that pretty on the payroll."

"What about the showgirls at the theater? Or the dancers in the gentlemen's club?"

"Nah, this one's on another level," he said. "Anyway, those girls live in a different world. You know what I'm saying?"

"No."

The bartender laughed cynically. "They live life in a bubble, always surrounded by losers trying to get a piece of 'em. To them, I'm just the help. I'm just the guy who calls the bouncer when someone's ruining their quiet drink at the bar."

"You sound bitter."

"I ain't." He brought two fingers to his temple and tapped it twice. "But I'm smart enough to know my place." He took one last glance at Payton's photo and then handed it back to

John. "As for your friend here, Vegas is a big town. It's easy to get lost here, especially if you don't want to be found."

~~~

Another hotel casino, another bartender.

"Try Tony in the Roman baths," a bartender at Caesar's Palace said. "He knows everybody. Second floor. Augustus Tower."

John left the Palace Tower and made his way through the Garden of the Gods Pool Oasis. The courtyard was empty, save for a few workers cleaning up around the faux Roman pools, whose turquoise waters were framed by palm trees, Italian cypresses, Roman columns and statues, and huge, empty urns. Vegas partied—and slept—hard. It was past 10 AM, but hardly anyone had emerged from their deluxe accommodations to bask in the blinding sunlight.

John spotted his reflection in one of the pools and realized he'd hardly taken a moment to breathe since he had woke up this morning. He paused to take in the opulence around him. For the first time that he could remember, Vegas felt cold—and a little sterile. And he knew why. Sin City looked like an elaborate shell game to anyone not caught up in the show. The opulence and the energy—everything about Vegas ran only skin deep. What lay beneath was anyone's guess.

Once inside Augustus Tower, John took the elevator to the second floor and poked around until he ran into a man in his forties wearing the Caesar's Palace insignia on his polo shirt. The guy was propped against one of the umbrella tables near the pool, slurping from a can of Red Bull.

"You Tony?"

"That's me. What do you need?"

"I'm Detective O'Meara with the New Orleans Police Department," John said and flashed his badge. "I'm looking for a missing woman and was told by a bartender over in the other tower that you know everybody in this town."

Tony laughed a husky laugh. He was a stocky guy, only

about five-foot-seven. But he looked like he could bust teeth, if need be. "I wouldn't go that far." He scratched his forehead. "You got a picture?"

"I do." John retrieved the photo from his wallet.

"She your sister?"

John nodded in surprise. "You're the first one to see a resemblance. She's my kid sister. Disappeared about three weeks ago. Said she'd found a new job. When she went job hunting, Caesar's Palace was on her list."

"I don't recognize her," Tony said as he squinted at the photo. "And I've got a photographic memory."

"Really?"

"Steel trap. I hope I'm not your last stop."

"No," John said and glanced down at the folded newspaper he was holding. "I've got one more on my list."

"Yeah? Where's that?"

"New place. I've never heard of it before. Dracula's Castle."

Tony coughed uncomfortably and then swigged his drink. "I tell you what, Detective. You could have saved yourself a lot of grief by going there first."

"What do you mean?"

"That joint's freaky. You should see the main act. If your sister found trouble, I bet she found it there."

CHAPTER 5

JOHN O'MEARA HANDED the taxi driver a ten-dollar bill and told him to keep the change. He was in Vegas after all, the land of the big tippers.

"Happy vamping," the driver said and pulled away from the curb before the detective could reply.

Above John loomed a Gothic tribute to Transylvanian lore, part fantasy, part spook show. Dracula's Castle, designed like a towering medieval fortress, began with an outer stone wall that was lined with turrets. Visitors drove through the main gate and parked in a vast sea of cobblestones. From there, it was a short walk to the drawbridge, where John now stood. Beyond the moat, which sparkled with fountain-fed water, loomed the castle itself.

In the sunlight, the castle looked tasteless and absurd—an inferior, plasticized substitute for the real thing. At night, with its soaring façade glowing above the footlights beneath it, it was just shy of awe-inspiring. It was still an exercise in camp, a monument to American kitsch, but its enormous silhouette jutting into the black sky fueled the imagination.

John's first visit, which was in the late morning, had been a replay of his trips to the other casinos. No one had recognized the photo of his sister. But John, unfamiliar with Sin City's latest uber-resort, had lingered long enough to catch a quick tour from the casino's assistant manager, a balding man with a handlebar mustache and a salesman's veneer. Though medieval on the outside, the castle played homage to strictly Vegas values on the inside. Lurking behind the moat was the hotel, including honeymoon suites in the tallest turrets; the bustling casino, which boasted hundreds of noisy slot machines as well as the usual games of chance; a posh restaurant, with a five-star menu and sticker-shock prices; a dinner theater, which was big enough to host national acts; and of course, a gentlemen's club, discretely tucked away behind the theater on the first floor.

"Come back tonight," the assistant manager had told John, "and meet Vladimir, our main act. He has his finger on the pulse of Las Vegas. If your sister has auditioned here or anywhere else on the Strip, Vladimir will know."

Whether the advice had been legit or simply part of the hard sell, John had decided to take the assistant manager up on his offer and return for another look. Maybe Vladimir would know something the others didn't.

He stopped in front of a bubbling black cauldron in Transylvania Lounge, where a girl dressed in a revealing black velvet robe was serving something steaming and, from the smell of it, 100-proof.

"Excuse me," he said to the medieval dominatrix, "can you direct me to Vladimir?"

"You a fan?" she asked cheerfully.

He flashed his badge. "Not exactly."

Her eyes narrowed. "He's at the bar," she said and pointed to a lanky, dark-haired gentleman sitting alone and nursing a drink.

"Thanks," John said and strode toward the bar, above which hung a collection of medieval maces.

Just as he reached the bar, the entertainer swiveled in his chair to face him. His eyes were bloodshot and an unhealthy shade of yellow, and he had the face of someone who'd just slept through the day. Not necessarily an attractive gentleman, but intriguing, if nothing else, and well dressed in a pair of black slacks and a black, silk shirt.

"You wanted to see me?" he asked in a thick eastern European accent.

"I—"

"Do not worry," he said and nodded to the girl serving the drinks from the bubbling cauldron. "I know who you are. Someone told me you would be coming. Your sister has gone missing?"

"Right," John said, feeling like he was now the one being questioned. He clumsily reached for his wallet to retrieve the photo of Payton. "She's been gone two weeks. She came here looking for a job before she disappeared."

Vladimir extended a pale hand, which was long and lean and spidery like the rest of him, and took the photo from John, eyeing him the whole time. "Can we talk while I eat, detective?"

"Sure."

"Good," Vladimir said. "My mind—everything is cluttered." He waved his hand in the air, as if he wanted to show the chaos in his head. "I think better on a full stomach, you see?" He set his drink on the bar and slipped off his stool, revealing a frame a good four inches taller than John's. "Come with me."

John followed him to a table in the corner lit by a candelabra, and a scantily clad waitress arrived with a pair of menus.

"He's not eating," Vladimir said and handed the menus back to her. "And you already know what I want." He turned to John. "I can't think until I eat. I can't *perform* until I eat. I go on in less than an hour. I must have my supper."

"Can I get you two something to drink?" the waitress asked.

Vladimir raised an eyebrow at John.

"I'll have a Blackened Voodoo with a Spanish accent," John said and waited for the waitress to ask for an explanation.

But she jotted down his order without question and turned to Vladimir.

"A Transylvania Martini for me," Vladimir said.

After a short wait, the waitress returned with John's beer, plus a dish of Spanish olives.

"I'm impressed," he said to her. "You didn't even have to ask."

"I'm a professional," she said nonchalantly.

Vladimir's drink was a black vodka martini with two spears of garlic floating in it.

John thought Vladdy boy's accent and getup were way over the top. This whole Transylvania vampire act was a hoot. Still, he decided to play along in case tall, dark, and weird had more information about Payton.

"How can you eat garlic?" John asked as soon as the waitress had left. "I mean, since you're a vampire and all?"

Vladimir laughed lustily. "But what about you? How can you drink that stuff? It looks like it came from the bottom of a swamp. It is so thick you need a fork to drink it. Come now, you will get a yeast infection if you drink that."

The detective came close to squirting beer through his nose. "I thought you were a magician, not a comedian."

"How do you Americans say? I do it all."

"You're not from these parts," John said, stating the obvious.

"No, and you are not allowed to laugh when I tell you my homeland."

"Okay."

Vladimir sipped at his martini. "Transylvania."

"As in Romania?"

"Ah, good. At least you know the country. Americans make lousy geographers."

"That's because we live at the center of the universe," John said.

"I dare say many of you honestly think so."

The waitress arrived and plopped Vladimir's meal in front of him: a bloody steak so rare it looked ready to bolt before the entertainer could stab it with his knife.

"Wipe its ass, blow its nose, and bring it out," John said in amazement.

"That is correct," Vladimir said. "My stomach is not pampered like yours. It needs real food."

"Whatever you say."

Vladimir sliced into the steak and licked his lips as blood pooled on the plate beneath it.

"You haven't looked at the photo yet," John said.

Vladimir stopped chewing and frowned. "Waitress," he said, calling her back to their table. "This is overdone. Please take it back and remind the chef who he cooks for."

The waitress rolled her eyes and disappeared into the kitchen with the steak.

"I apologize," Vladimir said. "How hard is it to lightly sear a steak?" The photo of Payton sat on the table beside his martini, and for the first time, he stopped talking long enough to study it. He shook his head solemnly. "I am sorry, detective. I do not recognize your sister."

"The assistant manager at the casino said you're well connected with the talent pool in Vegas," John pressed. "Do you know if she tried out at any of the other casinos or met with any booking agents or—?"

Vladimir shook his head and frowned. "Everyone thinks just because I am the most popular magician in all of Las Vegas that I know who's who. But detective, I kill one girl a night—two on Fridays and Saturdays. I cannot remember every girl I eat. You should stay for my act tonight. Then you will understand."

The waitress arrived with another steak.

"Damn," John said. "Looks like it went straight from the shrink wrap to your plate."

Vladimir smiled a toothy smile. "That is more like it."

~~~

It began like so many acts in Vegas—with an appetizer.

After John had been seated at a table for one at the back, the lights, already muted, were lowered further still. Crimson-toned shadows crept across the dinner theater's soft gold hues. The din of the sprawling casino, just a short stroll away, might as well have been on the other side of town. Here, the anticipation was more focused—and less likely to lead to heartburn.

"Can I get you anything else while you wait for the main course?" a Gothic beauty asked, her décolleté so revealing John felt compelled to look away.

"No thanks," the detective said, gingerly returning his gaze to hers. "If I'm not careful, I'm going to fill up on shrimp and beer."

The waitress laughed and then moved on to the next table.

Too cheerful, John thought, *to be working for a vampire*. She had the look down. She just needed to jettison the bright-eyed smile, which, though plenty flattering, contrasted wildly with her pale skin and black lips. *Needs to look more menacing*.

In fact, the first part of Vladimir's show was anything but.

The audience, made up mostly of forty and fifty-somethings, dined quietly as a band of gypsies entertained them with folk songs. The music, costumes, and dancing were all authentic, as far as John could tell, if a tad generic. He could have been in Romania for all intents and purposes, but he would have been watching a show staged by the Ministry of Tourism. The presentation felt too clean, too pretty, to jibe with what he imagined a lucky (and adventurous) tourist might stumble upon in a locals-only tavern somewhere in Eastern

Europe, the Old Country's last frontier, where folk songs were part of the cultural fabric, not a commodity.

With dessert—in John's case, another Blackened Voodoo—came a brilliant display of horsemanship from a quartet of riders onstage, each of whom could have passed for a medieval horseman readying for battle against the Turks on the plains of Hungary. The men wore stubble on their grim faces and pushed their horses hard on the broad but shallow stage, leading them through an elaborate routine while shouting out gruff commands in what, John presumed, was a Romanian dialect.

It was an impressive demonstration and brought the audience to their feet for the first time, but something in the air shifted when Vladimir finally took the stage. If the horsemen were gritty and authentic, he was smooth and elusive like a fleeting glimpse of something too extraordinary to be real. From the horsemen, John had felt raw energy. Dangerous, but a sight to behold. From Vladimir he sensed something darker. Something … slippery.

Dressed in all black and sporting a black cape lined with red velvet, Vladimir introduced himself as a vampire with a gambling problem. "I like to take chances on women," he told the audience. "But I have yet to meet Mrs. Right. The objects of my affection, unfortunately, always end up dead."

As Vladimir launched into his open monologue, John realized he didn't know what he was watching. Was this a magic show or a comedy routine? Fantasy or horror? The show had shifted from generic entertainment to raw spectacle to … what exactly?

Vladimir, whatever he was presiding over, was a brilliant showman. In no time, he had the audience hanging on his every word, laughing at his jokes, giggling even at his wry facial expressions. Every time he raised an eyebrow or cocked his head or let loose an ornery smile, he had the audience in stitches, especially the ladies, but his appeal was universal. The guy knew how to work a room.

As soon as the audience was good and loose, thanks in no small part to the Goth-styled waitresses making repeated rounds with drinks and refills in hand, Vladimir introduced his assistant, Sasha, a buxom brunette with legs a mile long and breasts that defied gravity. If Vladimir's illusions had been pure sorcery, Sasha's bustline had to be the work of a surgeon's. She was a thing of beauty, and her presence added another element—in this case, class and a touch of vulnerability—to the show.

As Sasha earned a warm welcome from the audience, Vladimir proceeded with a series of mind-bending illusions. The first, which he dubbed the Vampire's Ball, established him as a first-rate illusionist. After he asked Sasha to choose a member from the audience, he waltzed with the woman to a spooky cello piece, at one point levitating himself and his partner several feet above the stage—all the while appearing invisible in front of a towering wall of mirrors, each of which showed his partner but not him.

He picked the girl ahead of time, John thought. *And those aren't mirrors. They're video screens.*

But Vladimir, anticipating just such a critique, invited the audience to pick his next dance partner, and she, too, was soon airborne, not to mention the only one visible in the mirrors behind her.

John gaped at Vladimir and then the mirrors behind him, all of which showed the almost comical vision of the woman waltzing alone six feet above the stage.

How does he do it?

Each of John's theories—Vladimir was wearing special clothing; parts of the presentation had been filmed in advance; the woman had joined the stage with wires already affixed to her clothing; the mirrors were specially designed and strategically placed—fell apart in short order as Vladimir asked the audience to determine not only his next partner but where they would dance on the stage.

By the time Vladimir introduced his next illusion, which he said would consist of his transforming himself into a blue-black timber wolf and then trotting offstage, John had given up trying to get a line on the source of the illusions and had decided to just sit back and enjoy the show.

With the audience shaking their heads and laughing in wide-eyed amazement, Vladimir returned to center stage, a man once again, and nodded at Sasha to roll away the towering mirrors.

"Ladies and gentlemen," he said, obviously preparing to wrap things up, "I want to tell you how much I have enjoyed myself tonight, but honestly, it is hard to stand here and see you all laughing and carrying on and teasing me with so many bare necks. You are all just happy meals on legs to me."

The audience laughed.

"My kind, we have to work for our supper. There are no drive-through windows, no free lunches, no blood banks for creatures of the night. If it were not for the power of suggestion, I would go hungry." He motioned to a young woman seated at a table in front of the stage. "Madame," he said, "please join me onstage."

The girl, dressed in black slacks and a conservative top, shook her head no and slunk down in her chair.

"Please," he said. "Can't you see how hungry I am?"

The audience laughed as the girl cringed.

"Fine," Vladimir said. "If you will not donate your blood to the cause, then you will get on your knees."

Now even the girl was laughing.

Vladimir lowered his voice to just above a whisper. "On your knees, my beloved."

John leaned forward in his chair. He could feel the sudden tension in the room. The laughter was dead.

The smile of embarrassment disappeared from the girl's

face, and she pushed herself away from the table and stood up.

"On your knees," Vladimir whispered into his headset microphone, his voice suddenly sounding distant, almost tinny in John's ears.

She did as he ordered and knelt in the aisle with her back to the audience.

"Now," the entertainer said, "I want you to bark like a dog."

The silence was suffocating.

"Bark like a dog," he whispered.

The girl cocked her head back and barked.

John felt his eyes widen. What the hell was this? The girl, a shrinking violet before, was suddenly barking on command. Without shame. Without theatrics. Without a smile on her face. She was barking, as though this was serious business. She was barking like a dog.

Vladimir let her bark for a few more seconds and then waved his hand. "Somebody help that poor woman," he said.

John felt a quickening sensation in his ears, as if the air pressure in the room had just dropped, and just like that, the girl stopped barking. She covered her mouth in embarrassment, stood up, and hurried up the center aisle toward the exit, with a distraught friend chasing after her.

The audience, suddenly jolted back to reality, reacted in quiet confusion. Were they supposed to laugh? Jeer?

"Sasha," Vladimir said in a hushed voice. "I hunger."

The buxom assistant dutifully knelt before him.

"No, no, I need you closer."

She took her feet and turned with her face to the audience, pulling back her hair and revealing a long, sumptuous neck.

"I hunger," Vladimir repeated in a whisper.

As he spoke, the lighting onstage disappeared until only a red-violet spotlight encircled him and his assistant, their silhouettes throwing long shadows against the dark curtain behind them. His angular face no longer looked like it belonged to a quirky European magician-comedian. His eyes, round and slightly bulging before, looked deep set beneath a bulbous brow. His mouth, weak and ragged-looking before, hung open like a predator's jaw.

"I hunger."

His voice was so quiet, and the tension in the room was so palpable that when his elongated canines tore into Sasha's neck, the audience pulled back in shock at the sickening sound. Sasha's eyes widened in disbelief, and she pushed against Vladimir's chest. But he gripped her even more viciously as he gulped at her neck, blood squirting like a geyser across her white blouse.

The two stood still in a grisly embrace, and John felt himself squirming in his seat. *Enough already*, he thought. *This isn't funny anymore.*

Slowly the color drained from Sasha's face until she was staring glassy-eyed at the audience. She was either a damned good actress or dead. The ghoulish, gray color spreading across her skin was one John knew all too well from his day job.

Finally, the spotlight dimmed, and the curtain fell.

The audience sat in numb silence. What had they just witnessed?

Someone near the front started clapping, and soon, he was joined by a few others and then more until everyone had taken to their feet and cheered wildly. A rough-edged Sex Pistols song began blaring from the overhead speakers, and the houselights came on. Vladimir, who held hands with a very alive-and-well Sasha, retook the front of the stage for a Shakespearean bow.

John looked down at his hands and saw that he, too, was clapping. *What the hell?*

Vladimir and Sasha disappeared behind the curtain once more, and the show was over.

~~~

It had to be the beer, John thought as he left the theater. The ringing in his ears, the all-too-real gore unleashed on stage—none of it had been real. Just smoke and mirrors. He felt his head swim. *I need another drink.*

He spotted the entrance to the gentlemen's club on his way out and decided to try to numb the agitation he felt in his gut. Vladimir was good. Damn good. He could see why the guy was one of the hottest tickets in town, but his act was more than PG. It bordered on the sinister. There had been so many uncomfortable moments. So many points where he had felt out of control, as though he hadn't known what he was actually watching. The worst of it—he hadn't flinched at the horror; he had enjoyed it.

He could hear a house mix blaring inside the gentlemen's club, and as he entered, he felt his mood lighten. The music could be felt as much as it could be heard, which right now was a good thing. He felt like he needed a freakin' exorcism. Or at least another Blackened Voodoo. As soon as he had paid the cover, he found a seat near the back and watched as two strippers worked their respective poles on adjacent stages.

"What can I get for you, honey?"

He pulled his eyes away from the strippers and smiled at the waitress in front of him.

"I'll have a—"

Wow. Who the hell is she?

Across the room on the other side of the bar and staring directly at him was the most devastating beauty he'd ever seen. She was dressed in satin black negligee just like the others, but she looked like a rose among spent daisies. She had a blue-black bob, straight out of Depression-era Paris, and a bewitching pair of eyes to kill for—or die for, whichever came first. Her beautifully pale skin looked like it had never been burned by sunlight. She was absolutely, unequivocally stunning. She was ...

"I'm waiting."

John remembered the waitress standing at his table. "Right. Sorry. I'll have a Blackened Voodoo."

"Coming right up," the waitress said and disappeared.

John nodded and then returned his gaze to the other side of the room, but the girl was gone. *Where did she go?* Not waiting for his drink, John rose and headed for the other side of the bar. He passed the two stages and the bar, everyone and everything in his peripheral vision nothing more than a blur, and hurried to where he'd last seen the phantom girl. He entered a small alcove and deliberated briefly in front of a pair of signs, one pointing the way to the restrooms and another in fancy script that read "Special Guests" before he chose the latter. He hurried down a long corridor and thought he caught a brief glimpse of the mysterious woman ahead of him.

A bald, beefy guy, a bouncer no doubt, stepped in front of him. The guy was about twice his size and reeked of garlic. His skin color was olive-toned, and he had a huge tattoo of a coiled snake on his left forearm. "Where you headed, partner?"

"I was——"

"You was what?"

"I was——"

"You wanna private dance, sugar?"

John whirled around to see a bleached-blonde woman with a fake-and-bake tan and surgically enhanced cleavage winking at him.

"Come on," she said. "Follow me."

He glanced at the bouncer and saw that he was still glaring at him and decided to follow the bleached-blonde, who led him to a small room.

She smiled at him. "Come on."

He followed her inside, and she shut the door.

"Don't mind the muscle," she said in what sounded like a New Jersey accent. "They're all bark and no bite."

"Right," John said. "Look, I——"

Before he could get the sentence out, the girl was undressed and writhing like a corkscrew in heat.

"Don't get all bashful on me now," she cooed. She tugged at his T-shirt and pulled him closer until their lips were only inches apart. "I'll give you a show you'll never forget."

In contrast to the bouncer's strong garlic breath, the bleached-blonde's smelled like iron. What was she doing? Cleaning her teeth with a cast-iron toothbrush?

John felt the same popping sensation in his ears that he'd felt back at the dinner theater, and the girl, all clingy and wiggly before, suddenly looked like something he'd seen at the Audubon Zoo. Her eyes had hoods, and her teeth were headed straight for his neck.

"Stop!" John yelled, pulling back and warding her off with his forearm.

She brushed off his forearm and slammed him against the wall.

Holy shit! That girl's a man!

He'd barely recovered from being tossed against the wall when he felt one of her high heels in his crotch.

He groaned and doubled over.

He felt his hair nearly being pulled out by the roots as she yanked his head back. And finally it hit him. As he stared into the man-girl's snakelike eyes, he realized he was looking at something that wasn't human. The throbbing in his ears was coming in waves now, one after another, and all he could hear was a screaming white hum.

"Get the hell off me!" he growled and sent the girl reeling with an elbow to her gut.

The blow threw her off balance, and he landed another one, this time smashing the palm of his hand between her eyes. Instead of delivering a knockout punch, he felt a shooting pain in his hand, like he'd just broken it in a dozen places.

"You like it rough," she said and smiled as blood dribbled down the bridge of her nose from a cut in her forehead. She dabbed at the blood with her forefinger and brought it to her mouth. "God, you make me hungry."

"What are you gonna do? Eat me?"

"Something like that."

She started toward him again, and suddenly, he remembered Vladimir's act. The ringing in his ears, the girl's inhuman transformation—was any of this real? He decided he didn't want to find out.

Before she could get any closer, he reached for his .45 and unloaded three rounds into her chest.

She staggered back, and a look of shock spread across her bemused face. "Ouch."

John felt the urge to pinch himself. This was the part where the perp was supposed to fall face first into the carpet, what with half of her insides splattered against the wall behind her. But she looked like she was just getting warmed up. He unloaded another round between her eyes and then bolted past her for the door, but it was locked—from the outside! He felt something clamp around his ankle and looked down to see the girl, blinded from the blood in her eyes, crawling on the floor and clawing at his feet. He kicked her away and then threw his shoulder into the door.

He groaned in pain. "How many times do I need to do that before I wise up?"

He backed away from the door and shot the doorknob loose, just enough to kick the door open and escape the girl's slithering hands.

"What the hell's going on?" The bouncer charged down the hallway toward him but slowed when he saw John's pistol aimed at his throat.

"Unless you've got a death wish," John hollered above the house music coming in from the bar, "you'll stop right there!"

The bouncer froze in his tracks. John stole a quick glance behind him and saw the girl was tangled up in the splintered door frame. He hurriedly returned his gaze to the bouncer. "Is there a back way out of here?"

The bouncer grudgingly pointed down the hallway with his eyes.

John emptied another round into the crazy girl and then hurried down the dark corridor. He worried for a split second that the bouncer had lied to him, that he had been herded into a dead end, but just when it looked like he was running out of real estate, he spotted an exit sign to his left and threw his weight against the door, the door opening this time.

He stumbled outside into what looked like a service alley, somewhere out back, the undecorated business side of Dracula's Castle. Would anyone follow? The bouncer? The stripper? He caught sight of the light coming from a streetlamp at the far end of the alley and, not bothering to catch his breath, ran toward it.

CHAPTER 6

"THERE'S NOTHING HERE."

John O'Meara stared in disbelief at the empty private booth. Less than an hour earlier, he'd been in the very same room, locked in mortal combat with some … thing. Now here he was, back at the scene of the crime with a Las Vegas police detective, staring at a clean room.

He glanced at the door and then the doorknob. Easy enough to replace. But what about the splintered frame? And what about the blood? He knelt down and touched the carpet with his fingertips. Was it moist? He couldn't tell. He sniffed at the air and thought he smelled a trace of vinegar.

He glanced up at Detective Oren Pettit, a gangly cop with a boxer's chin, who was gazing down at him with a condescending smirk.

"Like I said—nothing here. You sure this is the right room?"

"Let's check the alley," John said as he stood upright.

"You wanna go rummaging through dumpsters now?"

John rubbed his temples. He couldn't think straight. Where was the crazed girl he'd shot? And what about the phantom woman, the stunning looker whose image he couldn't get out of his head? He remembered the strange deadening sensation in his ears, and suddenly, images from Vladimir's gory show flashed in his mind: the glassy look in Sasha's eyes as the magician bit into her neck, the small river of blood streaking from her wound, and the red-violet spotlight casting everything in a surreal glow.

"No," John said, "if they can clean up a room this fast, I'm sure the evidence is long gone, but I doubt they got every trace. There's bound to be some bullet holes in the wall. At this range, my ammo would have passed right through that girl … uh, guy … uh, whatever it was. We need someone from forensics out here ASAP."

"Not gonna happen."

"What do you mean?"

"I mean, it's not gonna happen. You come into the station all bleary-eyed and smelling like a brewery and talking about bleached-blonde strippers turning into monsters. You drag me out here to see an empty room. And now you want me to tape this off as a crime scene and send in forensics? Ain't nobody at the station willing to stick their neck out that far for an out-of-town cop none of us know from Adam. And there ain't no judge in all of Vegas, not even a shotgun wedding specialist, who's gonna grant you the search warrant you need to come back. You're out on a limb, detective. I suggest you crawl back."

John resisted the urge to break his already throbbing right hand against Detective Pettit's jaw and instead removed his .45 and tried to hand it over to the detective. "Look, here's your first piece of evidence. It's half empty, and it was fired only an hour ago."

"Keep your gun," Detective Pettit said. "For all I know, you were unloading it at a shooting range." He scratched his angular chin. "I'll tell you what, detective. You give me a witness, and I'll file a report."

John thought for a moment. The girl he'd emptied half his magazine into? She was nowhere to be seen. The olive-skinned bouncer he had confronted? Gone. The hostess serving his beer? Gone.

The manager who had escorted him and Detective Pettit to the VIP room stood outside the doorway. He looked shocked and perplexed just as he had after he had heard John's brief retelling of his encounter. It was, the manager had told him after he granted his request to search the private booth, just another night at the club. The strippers had been doing their thing onstage, and the customers, though rowdy and lewd and stirred up like always, had been keeping their hands to themselves, at least as far as he could tell.

As John pondered what to do next, he remembered the look on the face of the girl just before she had attacked him. She had gone through some kind of creepy metamorphosis … just like Vladimir had onstage.

"I've got someone for you to bring in for questioning," John finally told Detective Pettit. "I'm sure he's lurking here somewhere."

~~~

John stood alone on the other side of the observation glass. Inside sat the magician whose show had marked the beginning of what was turning out to be another whacked-out night, the last in a long line for someone with a sick sense. He didn't have to go looking for weirdness, because it always came looking for him.

He was sober now, but his head pulsed, both from the pints of Blackened Voodoo he'd thrown back and from the freak show going on around him.

Vladimir, not surprisingly, was putting on quite a show in the interrogation room.

"What's your last name?" Detective Pettit asked.

"Frumos," the magician said in his thick accent.

"Where you from?"

"Transylvania."

"Ain't that a sweet coincidence? I bet you're from Russia.

Hell, you're probably from Cleveland. Just here to make a buck. Ain't no harm in that."

"You are free to believe what you wish," Vladimir said, looking bored. He glanced at the observation glass, as if he could see John. The guy was creepy in a tragically misunderstood kind of way, especially sitting under the small room's dingy yellow light.

"Frumos is an unusual name. What's it mean?"

"The handsome," Vladimir answered. "The lovely girls I eat on stage every night tell me the name is perfectly suited to its owner."

"I'm sure they do. So where were you about an hour ago?"

"Relaxing in the bar, right where you found me."

"Did you happen to see a detective from New Orleans named O'Meara?"

"I did. He came to see me before the show to ask about his missing sister."

"Missing sister?"

John felt his stomach leap. He hadn't wanted to look more desperate—or any less credible—than he already did. Thus, he hadn't shared that little tidbit with Las Vegas's finest. Now the cat was out of the bag.

"Yes, his sister has gone missing, apparently. Another shining star, come to Las Vegas to burn sweetly."

"What'd you tell him?"

"That I am unfortunately of no help. I did not recognize her photo. Our paths have never crossed. I would remember if they had."

"You like playing Dracula, don't you?"

"Of course. It is a wonderful act, don't you agree? But you must learn to distinguish between a man and his persona. The stage brings out the monster in me."

"Uh-huh. Detective O'Meara says you like blood-red steak and that your act looks more real than a crime scene. Says you drink martinis with garlic, too. Ain't that supposed to ward off vampires?"

Vladimir laughed from his belly. "Look, detective, the reason I got into showbiz is quite simple. I cannot endure sunlight. Therefore, a day job would never suit me. I suffer from porphyria. It is a very real and very debilitating medical condition. You are welcome to discuss the details with my personal physician. In the meantime, please tell me what I am doing here. Am I a suspect for some hideous crime?"

"Nope, just a potential witness."

"Well, I have seen nothing. I have heard nothing. I know nothing." He turned again to the observation glass and smiled a toothy smile. "Of course, this is not the first time I have fallen under suspicion, detective. Since I was a young boy living in my home village, I have been the object of scorn and suspicion from my neighbors. For my pale skin. For my aversion to sunlight. For my bloodshot eyes." He tugged at one of his ragged canines. "For my teeth. I am an entertainer, for pity's sake. All I have ever wanted to do is be onstage. Of what am I guilty? Please tell me."

"Nothing, as far as I can see." Detective Pettit sighed impatiently. "Detective O'Meara claims he was attacked by a stripper in a private booth at the gentlemen's club. Says she turned all vampy on him just like you did in your show. Maybe she was trying to copy your act."

"I find that highly unlikely," Vladimir said. "I share my secrets with no one. I do my own makeup. I am in charge of the special effects at my show. The stage hands know only enough to do their job, no more. I change assistants regularly in order to keep my secrets ... secret."

"Could someone watching you from the audience figure out how to pull off your transformation?"

"Never."

"How 'bout someone sneaking a peek from backstage?"

"As I said, everything I do is highly guarded. If it was that easy to mime, someone would have stolen my act by now. But I am an original."

"I'll say." Detective Pettit stood up. "Mr. Frumos, I'm sorry to have wasted your time. You're free to go."

Vladimir stood up and removed a card from his wallet. "If you need me again, I can be reached at the casino or at my penthouse downtown." He offered a formal handshake across the table to the detective. "You should come see my show."

"Sure as hell sounds like it."

Vladimir stopped at the door and threw one last glance toward John on the other side of the observation glass. "Remember, gentlemen, not to judge a book by its cover. And if your suspicions are justified, well, what then? Even monsters need to make a living."

~~~

"Missing sister, huh?" Detective Pettit asked.

"Yeah," John said.

"Did you file a missing person report?"

"No, I know how those things work,' John said. "It gets put on the bottom of the pile, and someone gets around to it—eventually. I wanted to look around myself."

"Look," said Pettit. "File the report anyway. And then pack your shit and go home. We'll take it from here."

The guy's smugness was too much to take, and John desperately wanted to wipe the condescending sneer from his face. Instead, he simply nodded as he left the observation room.

He stopped as soon as he was alone in the hallway. Now what? He was back to square one. Worse than square one. He had accidentally tapped into Sin City's dark side but still knew nothing of his sister's whereabouts. Now he had two problems instead of one.

Screw it, he thought and resumed walking. *Let Pettit deal with Vladimir. All I want is to find Payton—before her trail goes stone cold.*

But what if Vladimir was lying? What if Payton was somehow mixed up in whatever was going on at Dracula's Castle?

"Hey," someone said in a hushed voice.

John looked up to see a portly police officer standing between him and the exit.

"Do you mind if we talk?" the officer asked and glanced hurriedly down the empty hallway behind them.

John looked around. What was with the creeping paranoia? "Sure, but why are we whispering?"

The officer fumbled with a key ring full of keys. "Follow me," he said and led the way to a small supply room.

John entered behind him, and the officer hurriedly flicked on the light and then closed the door as soon as they were both inside.

"My name's Harry Feineman," the officer said, "but folks just call me Pudge."

"Nice to meet you, Pudge. Why are we hiding in the supply room?"

Pudge grabbed a stepstool and took a seat, his girth making the stool disappear. "Where do I start?" he asked.

"How 'bout at the beginning?" John said and leaned against a shelf stacked high with forms.

"Shoot, that'll take too long. I'll give you the skinny. I believe your story."

"And what story is that? I don't even know what just went on back there."

"The hell you don't. You were attacked by a vampire."

"Give me a break."

"Then what was she? A circus freak?"

John shook his head. "I don't know. I've seen people flying so high on crystal meth it took a shotgun to bring 'em down—and they never looked like her. She was positively whacked. Looked straight out of a horror flick."

"And just like Vladimir."

59

"Yeah, just like Vladimir."

Pudge motioned for John to grab the room's other stepstool. "Here's the deal. There's been a rash of disappearances lately, most of them women—*beautiful* women. Started six months ago, the same time Dracula's Castle opened and Vladimir debuted as their main attraction. I've got a list of the missing girls, seven in total, and all but one worked at the casino before they disappeared. If your sister auditioned for Vladimir, she could be his latest victim."

John bristled at the idea that he was already too late. "No way."

"Maybe not. But she could be in trouble—or tied up in this somehow." Pudge scratched at his double chin. "Whatever's going on, I think Vladimir is the key, and some pretty powerful people, whomever they are, have his back."

"What do you mean?"

"I mean, as soon as I started nosing around and puttin' two and two together, I got demoted to the desk by Chief Lowman."

"Lowman's your boss?"

"Uh-huh. He's a loudmouth who likes to hear himself chewing people out. Makes him think he's doing his job. He's got eyes and ears all over this place. I guarantee he already knows about you and your little adventure at the casino. Pettit's his favorite suck-up."

John tried to back the conversation up a few paces. "So are you telling me you believe in vampires?"

"Well, I haven't exactly seen one myself, but I've been reading through the lore ever since I connected Vladimir to the disappearances. Some of the Hollywood myths are accurate. Some are dead wrong."

"Such as?"

"Well, for starters, religious icons do nothing. In fact, a vampire can wear a cross without burning up. Holy water doesn't kill them. It only hurts them. And not because it's been consecrated. Any water hurts, which is why you won't see any vampires out in a rainstorm. Vampires hate water the way rabies victims can't stand it. And sunlight—they can't stand the sun."

John laughed. He couldn't believe he was having this conversation. "No rain. No sunlight. It's a wonder vampires ever get out."

Pudge's face turned a slight shade of red. "I know what you're thinking. This is all nuts. I thought so, too, at first. But what happened to you tonight? It's gotta make you wonder."

John remembered his private dancer. "I put enough lead in that stripper to send her to the morgue three times over, but she kept coming back for more." He shook his head numbly.

"That's because lots of things irritate a vampire, but from what I've read, only one thing will kill it."

"Let me guess: a stake through the heart."

"You got it. A vampire's only weakness is its heart. Putting a wooden stake through it—or remove it altogether—that's the only way to kill it. Shooting that stripper—all you did was slow her down. I guarantee she'll be dancing again in no time."

John opened his mouth to protest.

But Pudge was still jawing. "According to everything I've read, vampires have amazing recuperative power. You can use water or sunlight or even garlic to slow them down, but only one thing stops them for good."

John remembered the magician and his favorite drink. "Vladimir takes garlic in his martinis."

"Probably trying to build up a tolerance to it."

John leaned back on his stool, arms folded, and squinted skeptically at Pudge. "So how do vampires become ... vampires?"

Pudge nodded, as if he had anticipated the question. "Most victims are just that—victims. They're trapped. They die. But some are chosen for apprenticeships. The vampire sucks their blood but not all of it. Then he shares his blood with the victim, which completes the circle."

John thought of Sasha's death and resurrection onstage. "I assume you've seen Vladimir's act."

"I have."

"Do you think it's possible that his assistant—"

"Is already dead?" Pudge interrupted. "That's my theory. If she is a vampire, it would only take her a few seconds to recoup backstage before the curtain call. Hell, Vladimir could have a pint of blood waiting for her in the wings—or give her some of his."

"This is too freaky."

"You're right about that," Pudge said. He struggled to his feet and then handed John a piece of paper torn from a small spiral notebook. "Here's the name and number of someone who might be able to help you.

John glanced at the piece of paper with a telephone number and the name Angela Ramirez scrawled across it. 'Who is she?" he asked, frowning.

"A reporter for the *Las Vegas Sun*," Pudge said. "She covers politics. Get this," he murmured. "She thinks the mayor of Las Vegas is involved somehow with Vladimir and Dracula's Castle."

"Huh?" John asked.

"Yeah, she suspects the missing girls will be traced all the way to the mayor's office. I'm not so sure, but I know Vladimir is involved. If you go after him, maybe he'll lead you higher."

"'I don't know about calling a reporter, Pudge," John said. "I don't get along too great with reporters. They're too nosy and annoying. Know what I mean?"

"You're going to need all the help you can get," Pudge pressed.

"Guess so," John said, "but I'd rather just work with you."

"I can tell you everything I know. Give you a copy of the

file I started, assuming it hasn't been shredded. But I'm sort of … handicapped. The chief will have my nuts in a sling if I go chasing after this again."

"I understand." John stood up and followed Pudge to the door. "You need to keep a low profile. Otherwise, I lose my inside help."

Pudge stopped with his hand on the doorknob. "I'd rather not *disappear*."

"That makes two of us."

CHAPTER 7

JOHN WOKE UP Monday morning with something he hadn't had for several hours, namely a clear head. Vladimir's bloody show, the blonde bombshell turned ghoulish freak—there had to be a logical explanation for everything that had happened last night. Maybe Detective Pettit had been onto something. Maybe the stripper had somehow stolen Vladimir's act. Makeup and lighting could make anyone look spooky.

Of course, makeup and lighting couldn't account for how the stripper had thrown John around like a rag doll or explain how she had sustained multiple gunshot wounds, including one to the head, and still keep on fighting. But there had to be a logical explanation. Crack?

Today, in the broad light of day and without the dimming effects of too many Blackened Voodoos, John would get to the bottom of his mysterious encounter at Dracula's Castle. Why he had been stupid enough to drink on the job—something he never did back home—here in Vegas of all places, where excess and foolishness regularly ran amuck, was beyond him. It was time to pull his head out of his backside. Time to find his sister.

A taxi dropped him off outside the moat at Dracula's

Castle, and he hurried across the drawbridge toward the inner walls. Clarity had put a little something extra in his step.

I'm coming, Payton.

"Where're *you* going?"

John came to a stop in front of Detective Pettit and another plainclothes cop, both of whom were standing, arms folded, outside the casino's arched entrance. "Inside," he said.

The lanky detective shook his head no. "We figured you'd be back, which is why my boss called your boss back in New Orleans. Sounds like you're already on thin ice as it is."

That was a lie, or at least an exaggeration. Captain Whiting was a bit combustible at times but only because of the pressure he got from the city council and the press and everybody else. Yeah, he and John had gone at each other a few times, but the captain was a fair man who appreciated the detective's work. Most of the time, anyway. So long as he wasn't accidentally killing perps before they could be questioned. Or roughing up bad guys in front of news cameras. Or procuring evidence in creative ways.

"You're full of shit," he said, barely able to hide his venomous feelings toward Detective Pettit.

"Maybe," the detective said, "but your captain says if you want a job when you get back, you'll catch the next flight home. In fact, he requested we escort you back to your hotel, watch you pack, and put you on a plane—*post haste*, he said."

The jerk wasn't lying. *Post haste* was one of Captain Whiting's many stock expressions. John felt a creeping sensation closing in on him, as if everything was spiraling out of control. He had no leads on his sister. He'd come face to face with some freakish stripper. And now he was being sent packing.

"And if I refuse?"

"We get to cuff you and take you in," Detective Pettit answered quickly, practically spitting out the words. "I'm hoping you'll refuse."

John felt enough anger welling inside him to burn

Dracula's Castle to cinders. He wanted nothing more than to erase Detective Pettit's smirk permanently, but he was beaten. For the moment, at least. One thing he had learned over the years was how to pick his battles. This one, as tempting as he found it, wasn't worth fighting.

~~~

"Shut the door," Vladimir said. "It is time we talk, you and I."

Sadie narrowed her eyes at the magician, who was sitting in front of his dressing room mirror with the bulbs dimmed and his face in the shadows. The vanity of the man bordered on the absurd. What in hell's name did he need a mirror for? And who was he playing to now? His makeup artist? She wouldn't be here for hours. The imaginary audience in his head?

"You're in awfully early," she said, straining to be polite. "Shouldn't you be in bed trying out one of your new assistants?"

Oops. Every impulse she had told her to go after the man's throat.

"Charming, as always," Vladimir said. "You make it impossible to forget your razor-sharp wit. But what of you? What brings you into the light of day? I would think you, too, would be sleeping off another one of your ... adventures."

"Couldn't sleep," she said tersely. The last thing she wanted to do was talk about her problems with Vladimir.

"Join the club, darling. It seems I have an unlikely pair of admirers, including a rather bullheaded detective from New Orleans. What's more, I keep hearing distressful reports on your latest exploits, which I'm sure you are aware leave the powers that be twitching fitfully. We all admire your work, Sadie darling, but there are those who worry you'll be the death of us all."

Sadie shrugged. "What do you want?"

The question was only a second old, but she already regretted it. She watched as Vladimir stood up, his gangly frame towering above hers, and she felt his mind instantly at work on hers. He would always want her, and she would always regret the day she had met him.

"You know what I want," he said, toying with one of the spaghetti straps holding her minidress in place. He lowered the narrow strap and then the other until all she could feel against her skin was the cool draft of the air-conditioning.

She raised her hand against his chest. "No pudding for you," she cooed, "until you tell me what *else* you want."

The magician, normally so in control, looked positively bewitched and was clearly having a difficult time keeping his eyes to himself.

She sucked in her already taut tummy and raised her eyebrows, waiting.

"I—" he floundered. "I want you to keep an eye on someone for me."

"Who might that be?"

"An Officer Harry Feineman of the Las Vegas Police Department."

"What about your boy from New Orleans?"

Vladimir waved at the air. "He is not your concern, but this Feineman fellow—he has been talking to the press and anybody who will listen. The man has a big mouth but no friends in the department."

"Meaning?"

"Meaning that you should be careful and discreet, as always. But not so cautious that you fail to act. No one important will notice when he goes missing."

"I see. So I'm your errand girl now, am I?"

Vladimir frowned impatiently. "We all chip in where we can."

"See, Vladdy, that's where you're wrong. You're assuming I want to be a part of the team." She spit the last word out as derisively as she could.

The magician raised an eyebrow. "What sort of nonsense is this?"

Sadie glanced away momentarily, and then after she exhaled coolly through her teeth, she fixed her gaze on her former mentor. "Just me being me. You might be comfortable sacrificing for the team, but count me out. I work for no one."

"That is not true," he protested. "You work for me, and I work for the powers that be. Perhaps I have to make the occasional sacrifice in order to keep my name in lights, but I do it for my art. I do it for you, for all of us."

Sadie shook her head. "You really believe that shit, don't you?"

"Of course. I—" Vladimir checked himself. "No more silly talk, my love. I have given you your assignment, and you will make good on your obligation to me. Now ... let us move on to more important things."

Since her induction into Vladimir's shadowy world, Sadie had sunk to previously unimaginable depths, but there was a power in death, a power in having lost everything. She was free to be whomever she wanted, to live however she pleased. Yes, she was still working it all out. Sometimes, she felt like a human wrecking ball, ready to lay waste to the weak and the timid. Other times like now, she felt lost. She felt the way she did after a kill. Satiated yet still empty. Avenged but still waiting for redemption. There was something inside her, deep within and still largely untapped, that was determined to find another way, *her* way. Maybe she was a monster, but she didn't have to be a *kept* monster. She sure as hell didn't have to be Vladimir's errand girl.

She slowly bent to her knees and retrieved her minidress, which lay in a crumpled heap at her feet. As she pulled it over her head, she noticed something she hadn't felt for weeks, a sliver of independence. For the first time since she'd lost it, her heart felt remarkably untangled—almost free.

"Listen, Vladdy," she said as soon as she was dressed, "I don't feel like playing today, okay?"

If she'd had a camera, she would have captured the bewildered look on the magician's face for posterity. Instead, she made a quick exit while he was still picking his jaw up off the floor.

~~~

Angela Ramirez settled into her chair and opened a file on her desktop. As she studied her notes, she came to the unsettling but unavoidable conclusion that there wasn't enough here to break the story wide open—not yet.

"Hey," a voice interrupted her thoughts.

She looked up to see her editor, Sam Farmer, staring down at her with a smirk on his lips. He had his arms folded and was leaning against the entrance to her cubicle. Farmer stood only about five-foot-eight on a good day, but he commanded a great deal of respect, not to mention a fair share of fondness, from his reporters. He boasted an outsized personality, heavy on charisma and overflowing with energy, and he spoke as well as he wrote. Simply put, his command of language was elegant with gravitas. Aging seemed to do nothing but bring out his finer qualities. Despite the fact that he was pushing sixty, he possessed a ruggedly handsome face with a strong chin and steel-blue eyes partially obscured by an understated pair of wire-rimmed glasses. The man could look thoughtful one moment and mischievous the next, and his wry grin kept Angela constantly guessing.

"Hey, boss. What's up?"

"Nothing much. Just checking in with my ace reporter."

"Oh." She looked away self-consciously. "I suppose you want to know how the story on the mayor is going."

"You suppose correctly," he said with a wink. "What's the latest?"

"Still nothing sticking."

"The Teflon Mayor rides again."

"Right."

Had Mayor Randall A. Ward owned a different last name, he would have been ridden out of town on a rail by now, considering the ethics investigation opened against him a year earlier. The fact that he had weathered the perfect political storm and somehow won reelection proved, if nothing else, the iconic status attached to his last name. The Ward family had a pedigree a mile long and a rich history of political service in Nevada. They were the Kennedys of Vegas. The mayor's staying power also proved that Vegas voters, for all their unpredictability, were not easily swayed by alleged ethical problems, even if those problems were being investigated by the office of the state's attorney general.

Mayor Ward was being investigated for bribery, cronyism, and lobbying violations, among other things. According to the attorney general, who happened to belong to the mayor's rival political party, the mayor, if indicted and convicted on one of any of the serious charges currently being explored, could face up to ten years in prison, in addition to paying three hundred grand in fines, give or take a few thousand dollars. If the allegations were true, then they would mean that he had accepted cash gifts from certain businessmen in exchange for influence with his office; he had brought in unqualified people for important (and traditionally nonpolitical) positions, even fast-tracking friends' business projects; and he had accepted an all-expenses-paid trip to the Bahamas in exchange for listening to select lobbyists and endorsing their causes.

But for the moment, the details of those allegations were sealed and confidential, not to be divulged until the case—or rather, cases—went before a judge.

Thus, Angela, the reporter at the *Las Vegas Sun* doing most of the heavy lifting on the developing story, had been forced, at least in the early months after the stuff began hitting the fan, to run carefully parsed stories short of analysis and chock full of competing quotes from the mayor's attorney and the attorney general's office.

Predictably, the public had shown little interest in the story until sex had entered the picture. Mayor Ward was a married man after all—and a champion of family values. Six months into the ethics investigation, an intern working in the mayor's office had aired allegations of extramarital affairs between the mayor and at least three women, one of whom had allegedly been paid hush money to keep quiet. The mayor, inches away from being indicted in the attorney general's ever-widening probe, suddenly looked vulnerable. But before any of the charges could gain traction—and before any of the claims could be substantiated—the intern, Tina Porter, had gone missing. After they searched her apartment and found her computer trashed, her desk raided, and her walls vandalized, the police had come up empty, with Chief Lowman defying all logic and declaring it a garden-variety burglary, most likely unrelated to the intern's disappearance.

Despite the growing laundry list of complaints against the mayor, he was still in office, still doing business as usual, albeit with the vultures circling above.

"What about the missing girls' case?" Farmer asked. "Are you still working with someone at the police department?"

"He was pulled from the case," she answered. "I'm still in touch with him, and he's doing what he can. But—"

"Any chance of making headway with someone else?"

"With the LVPD? Not likely. My guy's the guy. No one else will talk to me."

"That's surprising," Farmer said and removed his glasses to inspect them. "Seems like the police are pretty good at leaking information."

"When it works to their advantage," Angela said. "In this case, they're maintaining pretty good discipline."

"Well, what are you working on now?"

"Just waiting for word from the attorney general's office on whether the indictment is going forward or if they're waiting for more evidence."

Farmer cleaned his glasses on his tie and returned them to his nose. "Well, that will be the first in a long line of big stories, assuming everything moves forward. Any chance the attorney general decides not to indict?"

"Sure," Angela said. "There's always a chance, but if I were the mayor, I wouldn't count on it."

~~~

Mayor Randy Ward glanced at his watch and then across the table at his lawyer, Cunningham. *Why does he have to be so dramatic? Can't he see I'm busy?*

Finally, the slim lawyer spoke. "It doesn't look good, sir."

The mayor motioned for him to be more specific. "Go on."

"Well, between the trip to the Bahamas and the cash gifts, not to mention the unusual appointments and the creative bookkeeping, if they go after that, you could do significant jail time."

"When you say significant—"

"I'm talking years. Maybe even in the double digits, if the judge is a stickler."

"Judge? So you think an indictment is a foregone conclusion?"

Cunningham exhaled through his mouth slowly and then tossed his pen onto his notepad. "Yes."

The mayor felt a surge of anger, but it spent itself quickly. It was tempting to fault the media or the state attorney or the fact that his state was largely run by the other political party, but he knew he had no one to blame but himself for his troubles. He had always championed conservative values to his loyal followers: honesty, integrity, hard work, a life of faith. But he had let himself be steamrolled by special interests, special projects, special relationships—the list went on. From his first day in office, everyone had wanted a piece of him. Those who had helped elect him quickly came calling, each with a pet project or favor they expected in return for their support. Who was he to say no? At the time, he had justified his ethical lapses by focusing on the ends, not the means. When that didn't work, he tried to remind himself that his intentions were good, that he truly cared about the people of Vegas and had their best interests at heart.

However, his inner guilt had found a way to be heard. A nagging anxiety had morphed into raging panic attacks and an addiction to tranquilizers. And his optimism, sunny and robust, had disappeared entirely, replaced by a sort of reckless fatalism. As each new revelation about his misconduct was printed in the local media, he let himself careen a little more out of control. He no longer tried to hide troubling associations, and he no longer cared what others did to protect or extend the widening circle of transgressions. He knew just enough to know that his problems belonged to others now, criminals and victims alike. Corruption, like a serpent eating its own tail, had a habit of feeding on itself, of growing exponentially. There were others who wielded their power in more traditional—and more brutal—ways. What they had done behind closed doors in his city would likely see the light of day someday, and he would be judged accordingly. His fate was in their hands.

He looked down at *his* hands, small and soft, the hands of a politician, and he felt nothing but self-loathing. A storm was coming his way, and he was powerless to stop it.

~~~

As soon as John's plane touched down and he found his baggage, he retrieved his car and headed straight to the office. He wanted to talk to Whiting—post haste. Captain James Whiting, or Jimmy as his closest associates called him, had a kind face, with a bald head and a pair of ears that looked ready for takeoff. His voice sounded like it belonged to a blues singer or a two-pack-a-day smoker. Perpetually hoarse, he always made sure his employees shut the door behind them as soon as they entered his office so he didn't have to raise his voice. This afternoon's visit from John was no different.

"Close it," he croaked and waved at the door.

John did as he asked and then took a seat across from him, the captain's enormous oak desk separating them by a good six feet.

"Do you want me to explain, or do you want to skip straight to reading me the riot act?"

Captain Whiting coughed out a laugh. "You know that's not my style, John. Then again, I gotta say I'm still having a hard time believing that one of my detectives would be stupid enough to step on another city police department's toes."

"I—"

Captain Whiting raised his hand to cut him off. "I heard all about it. Every gory detail, including the part about you allegedly emptying half your gun into a lap dancer at a strip club—and then not being able to dig up so much as a witness afterward, unless you count some freak magician from Transylvania. How do you do it? I really wanna know. How do you manage to find trouble wherever you go? How do you go to Vegas and dig up a vampire ring?"

Until now, John had enjoyed an unspoken pact with his captain. Everybody knew about his uncanny habit of unearthing spooky situations. The captain had to know the rumors. Had to have heard the stories. But neither he nor John ever spoke about the unspeakable. They kept things strictly professional. Now his boss was crossing that divide.

"Listen, Jimmy," John said, not sure how to proceed. "I didn't go to Vegas to cause trouble. I just went there to find my sister."

"Yeah, I know all about Payton, too, mister. And I tell you what—you'd be a lot further along with your investigation by now had you gone through proper channels instead of spending your weekend chasing ghosts."

"Vampires."

"Right. Vampires. What's next? Werewolves? Zombies? Witches? Why can't you just bust ordinary criminals?"

"It's a curse."

"No shit. You and your sick sense."

John decided to lay his cards on the table. "Look, sir, with your permission, I'd like to take a week off and—"

"Oh, no, you don't. You're staying right here, where I can keep an eye on you."

"And leave Payton to the wolves? No way."

Captain Whiting tossed a form across the desk. "Of course not. You're going to fill out this missing persons report and send it to the Vegas PD. Then you're going to help them do their jobs by staying out of their way."

Another no-win situation. John clinched his teeth and stood up. "Are they going to report to you?"

"Damn straight," the captain said. "Let me do the riding. I'll make sure they stay on the case."

"We're talking about my kid sister, Jimmy. She's all I got."

"I know," Captain Whiting said. "We'll find her. I promise."

~~~

Failure tasted like bile. Like something he couldn't force himself to swallow, no matter the circumstances. As John pushed the door open to his apartment, he resolved to find a way around the Las Vegas Police Department and around Captain Whiting, who was playing it by the book while Payton's life hung in the balance. It might take him a day or two to work it out, but he had to find a way back to Vegas. *A day or two.* The thought made his jaw harden. Every minute—every second— counted. For all he knew, his sister was standing at death's door. Had she auditioned for Vladimir? What happened to the magician's assistants as soon as they had been rotated out of his show? He thought of Pudge and his file on the missing girls. He would start there first.

He heard a scraping sound and froze in his tracks. *What now?*

The sound was coming from the kitchen. A thief? His mind leapt at the possibilities. Had someone from Dracula's Castle followed him back to New Orleans? He drew his gun and silently clicked off the safety. Whoever it was clearly hadn't heard him enter, because the same scraping sound was growing louder.

He stepped lightly toward the kitchen, hugging the entryway wall as he closed in on the intruder. He would have to act fast. *Damn*, he thought. *I don't want to make a mess!* If he could disarm whomever it was that was in his kitchen without shedding blood. Ah hell, that meant wrestling someone to the floor, someone possibly armed and more than likely dangerous. To hell with that. A little blood on the floor was better than getting himself killed.

He sprang into the open doorway, gun at the ready.

"You!"

"Hey, babe."

There she was, dressed in another one of his shirts—this time a plain black T-shirt. He had to admit that she looked a hell of a lot better in it than he did.

"So," Jenny said, "is this how you greet all your live-in lovers?"

"I—"

She placed the cheese grater she had been holding on the counter and stepped to within an inch of his loaded gun, which was still aimed squarely at her beautiful chest. Her smile was still the same: disarming, devastating, delicious.

John lowered the .45 and reengaged the safety. "I thought you were someone else."

"Obviously," Jenny said and drew a step closer.

He could smell chocolate on her breath.

"What have you been eating?"

"Hershey kisses. I found your stash in the cupboard. I

would have saved you some if I'd known you were coming back tonight." She bit her lower lip. "I kind of, you know, have been staying here since you left. I tried going back to my place, but I didn't make it past the front door. I feel safer here."

Three days worth of tension suddenly released from John's shoulders. His neck, bristling moments before, felt damp from sweat. "You know, kid, I think I missed you."

"Me too," she said and kissed him softly. "It's awful quiet here. I've had to resort to listening to your neighbors argue."

He returned her kiss. "You can stay here as long as you need, but eventually, we need to get you back on your feet."

"I know," she said. "I promise I won't wear out my welcome."

"That," he said, warming to her arms around his neck and her body pressed against his, "would be awfully hard for you to do."

She cocked her head to the side and smiled knowingly. "Officer, you look like the cat that just swallowed the canary."

"*Detective.*"

"Whatever. You look like you're ready to pounce."

"Almost," he said and glanced at the cheese grater on the counter and a small mountain of cheddar. "What've you got going there?"

"Quesadillas. I had to be creative. Your refrigerator is about as empty as my stomach."

"Why don't we go out to eat? After—"

"After what?"

"After we get reacquainted."

CHAPTER 8

AT THE FIFTH District precinct the next morning, John slouched in his chair until his head was even with the computer monitor staring back at him. He hated sneaking around, not because he was afraid of getting caught, but because it wasn't in his nature to hide. He preferred to wage his battles in the open. Pretending to be busy while actually chasing down his sister's whereabouts didn't just feel deceitful. It felt cowardly.

It also felt like a farce. Captain Whiting had to know what he was up to. When was the last time he had spent this much time pushing paper? Everyone at the department had a cubicle, or at least a desk and a phone. Most of the guys had photos on their desks of their wives and kids. Calendars with notes scrawled on them. Post-it notes. Billy Thune, his best friend at the department, had potted plants in his cubicle for crying out loud. All John had was an unused computer and a desk buried under a mountain of paperwork. His office—if you could call it that—was his car, away from the clutter and politics of so much brass. As far as Billy and the others were concerned, John didn't even know how to turn on his computer, but here he was, filing months-old paperwork, dusting off his keyboard, and even checking his e-mail. He had spent twenty minutes figuring out how to set up his voice mail, another half hour reviewing the latest policy directives to make their way down the chain of command, and now his chance had finally come. With the captain breaking in a couple of newbies in his office, it was time to get on the horn.

"Pudge," he whispered, "you got a second?"

"O'Meara?" Officer Feineman answered. "Is that you? I can barely hear you."

"I'm on the clock," he said tersely.

"Got it. Me, too. You want the latest?"

"Give me the skinny."

"Caucasian male in his mid- to late forties. Found early this morning buried in the desert about twenty miles outside of Vegas. Body barely cold."

"Who found him?"

"Birdwatcher. The guy did time in Vietnam. Knew right away he was looking at a hastily dug grave."

"Any leads?"

"Nope. The perps covered their tracks well."

"Have you seen the body?"

"Just the photos. No sign of foul play, other than some bruises—and a pretty gruesome bite wound on his neck."

"Vampire."

"So you're finally willing to admit it?"

"No. Just figured that was your theory."

"Still in denial, eh?"

"Just trying to keep one foot in the sane world."

"Don't worry, detective. I don't see a rubber room in your future."

"Of course not. You're already there. Do you think this is related to the missing girls?"

"Well, now that's the funny thing. Mr. Birdwatcher took it upon himself to start looking, and low and behold, he found four other graves nearby, all with the same MO, although much older. Three pretties, one stiff. Once the dental ID's come in, I guarantee we'll know what happened to at least three of Vladimir's beautiful assistants."

"Are they bringing him in for more questioning?"

"Nope. He's not a suspect, as far as I know. Mind you, they're keeping me at arm's length on this one."

"Payton—" John said but didn't finish the sentence. He couldn't even finish the *thought*. He had a pit in his stomach wide enough to drive a hearse through.

"She's not one of 'em," Pudge said in a reassuring voice. "She hasn't been gone long enough. From the sounds of it, the bodies with the exception of the first one were well on their way to decomposing."

"You'll keep me posted?"

"Damn straight."

"In the meantime—"

Pudge finished his thought. "I'm faxing you everything I've got: official reports, newspaper clippings, my notes. Everything I put together before Lowman kicked me downstairs. The bastard didn't even want my file."

"At least he didn't make it go away."

Pudge sighed thoughtfully. "I never thought about that. I guess we're lucky."

"Luckier than those girls."

"Don't forget about the stiff."

"Right. He was pushing up the same cactuses."

"One more thing."

John was starting to like Pudge. He was helpful, *and* he didn't waste words. "What's that?"

"Remember that reporter I told you about?"

"Yeah."

"You'll probably be angry with me, but I told her about your sister and that you're trying to track her down."

John felt his muscles tense. So much for Pudge being helpful. "What for?"

"I figured you wouldn't bother calling her. Now maybe she'll call you. She's really a crackerjack reporter."

"Maybe, but she doesn't carry a gun, and I prefer to work solo."

"Is that what you're doing now?"

John laughed quietly. "You caught me. I'll call her if I get a chance."

"Liar."

John gave Pudge his fax number and then sat up straight in his chair long enough to see the blinds in the captain's office being opened. The meeting with the newbies was breaking up, or close to it.

"Gotta go, Pudge. It's about to get crowded in here."

"Be safe."

"Right back at you."

John was tucking the documents from Pudge's fax into a manila folder just as Captain Whiting and the green officers emerged from their powwow. Thanks to Pudge, he'd have plenty of homework to study tonight back at his apartment.

~~~

"Congratulations on your big break," Vladimir said as he joined the girl onstage. "What is your name?"

"Lucy!" she squealed. "I'm so excited!"

Hardly eighteen, Lucy had been carefully vetted in human resources and then again by the casting director. Bubbly, wide-eyed, and built with long legs and ample curves, she had everything going for her. She turned heads just as she had at her audition. More importantly, she was capable of change—*radical* change—without anyone taking note, for she was new to the desert. She had no friends. No family. Just a starry-eyed exuberance for everything Vegas had to offer. If someone from her former life were to pay her a visit, they would no doubt notice the transformation, but they would likely attribute it to her line of work. Showbiz, as everyone knew, changed people. It made them slick. It made them cynical. It made them shallow and self-serving. And more often than not, it brought out their dark side.

In short, the long-legged redhead staring back at him with sky-blue eyes and a permanent smile was perfect for the job.

With the curtains drawn and the front doors to the theater locked, Vladimir had her to himself—more or less.

"Sadie, darling," he called backstage, "are you ready to meet the new girl?"

Lucy smiled nervously as she waited beside Vladimir, her hand trembling with excitement.

Vladimir tried to reassure her. "Sadie is always late, but do not fret. She is a professional."

Lucy bit her lower lip anxiously. "So … like, where are you from, exactly? Canada?"

Vladimir laughed from his belly. "Close enough, my young entertainer."

Finally, Sadie arrived, striding up the ramp to the stage in a midnight blue crushed velvet pantsuit with a long tail in back and the buttons in front half undone, revealing a lacy black bra beneath. As usual, she had managed to make what she was wearing look like a negligee, which was one of her many specialties.

Vladimir stole a glimpse of Lucy's face and spied the same jealousy that Sadie seemed to inspire in all women. She was, for better or worse, a steamroller in high heels. Strangers and intimates, clients and coworkers—everyone in her path ran the risk of being flattened by her sheer beauty. As his original assistant, she had stuck with the show for several months, bedazzled, at least initially, by his Old World charms and dark ways. But even vampires sometimes lost, and he could sense he was losing her now. She had always been beautiful and the owner of a sharp intellect even before she had become his first protégé, but the admiration and respect she had shown him in their early days together had turned to dust. In its place, he felt nothing but friction. He sometimes wondered what she had expected when he had first promised her immortality. Love? Happiness? She had to know by now that living forever came at a price.

"Your new toy?" she asked coldly.

Vladimir feigned shock at the remark for Lucy's benefit, not Sadie's. "Please excuse her," he said to the young girl. "Sadie works countless hours toiling on our behalf. She is indispensable, if a tad irresponsible."

"Yeah, yeah," Sadie said. "Let's get this show on the road." She unbuttoned her crushed velvet jacket the rest of the way and tossed it nonchalantly to the stage's bouncy wood floor. "Don't want to get blood on it," she said, looking and sounding utterly bored.

"Blood?" Lucy asked.

"Not real blood, of course," Vladimir said and directed her by her arm to the center of the stage. "But messy, nevertheless."

Lucy glanced back at Sadie and then whispered to Vladimir, "What's up with her?"

"Oh, nothing to worry about," he whispered back. "Just a little overworked. Now," he said aloud and clapped his hands together, "let's get started. As I am sure you are aware, my act is one of comedy and illusions, adventure and … horror." He smiled decorously. "Sadie is here for your initiation. But before I walk you through the paces, I'd like you to join us in a little … fun."

"What kind of fun?" Lucy asked. She looked suspiciously from Vladimir to Sadie, who was waiting stage left with her hands on her hips.

Sadie ran her tongue along her upper lip. "The best kind of fun," she said, answering for Vladimir.

Lucy's blue eyes narrowed. "Are you saying what I think you're saying?"

Vladimir stepped in. "And what do you think we are saying?"

"Well," she drawled, "it sounds like you wanna do something kinky." She threw up her hands in protest. "No offense, but I hardly know either of you—and no one said anything about sex."

"Sex?" Sadie said and drew closer, her hips churning slow and seductive. "Who said anything about sex? We just want to eat."

Lucy searched the empty stage, confused. "Eat? I'm not really hungry."

Sadie opened her mouth, no doubt to set the young girl straight, but Vladimir cut her off. "My young apprentice," he said to Lucy, "showbiz is all about giving. You give something to me. I give something to you. If you want to join my act, you will have to be, as you Americans say, a 'team player.'" He cocked his head, wondering if his hunch was correct. "Have you actually seen my act?"

Lucy pulled her lips together in a tight frown and looked away. "Not exactly."

"So much the better," he said with a laugh. "If nothing else, today will be instructive for you."

With that said, he paused to relish the moment. This was by far his favorite point in the routine. Just like the others had been before her, Lucy was positively in the dark about what was to become of her. Soon, she would be no different than any of the countless assistants that had preceded her: a consummate victim, a world-class *drainee*. But the first time was always the worst. If she was anything like the others, she would thank him as soon as she was breathing again.

"I personally would always recommend watching an act and thoroughly studying it before you decide whether or not you wish to play a part," he finally said. "But you, Lucy, are what I would call brave. Isn't she brave, Sadie?"

"Whatever," Sadie said. "Can we eat now?"

~~~

The girl on the screen let loose a bloodcurdling scream.

"How can you watch this stuff?" John asked from the kitchen table, where he was reviewing Pudge's notes.

Jenny was snuggled up on his futon in front of the TV and engrossed in a horror flick. "Therapy," she said without taking her eyes off the action.

John shook his head. If he didn't make some headway on Payton's disappearance soon, he was going to need treatment himself. Pudge had been right about the overall picture, which pointed back to Vladimir or at the very least to Dracula's Castle. Seven Vegas-area women, each of them exceptionally beautiful, had disappeared in the last six months. At the time of the disappearances, all but one had been working at the casino. The one exception, Tina Porter, a senior at the University of Nevada, Las Vegas, had been volunteering as an intern at the mayor's office. If Pudge was right, the remains of three of those women were chilling right now in a morgue in Vegas.

The byline on most of the news clippings Pudge had filed away belonged to a reporter by the name of Angela Ramirez. John glanced at the card Pudge had given him back at the station supply room in Vegas and made a match. So this was the journalist Pudge wanted him to contact? Pudge was right. Her reporting was rock solid, not to mention aggressive. As it turned out, the mayor was embroiled in his fair share of political controversy. The fact that one of his interns had gone missing threw new suspicion his way. Ms. Ramirez had gone so far as to suggest a possible link between the intern's disappearance and the others'. No other reporter had offered analysis so bold.

But what about the two male bodies—one fresh, one old—found this morning in the desert? How did they fit in? According to Pudge's notes, a handful of men had disappeared in Vegas in the last six months as well, but their vanishing acts had not caused much of a stir. Most had been tourists or business types—the very people who might have been hanging out at a casino—but others had been average locals with no discernible qualities in common.

John reached for his cell phone and punched in a Vegas area code and phone number.

"Hey," he said as soon as Pudge answered. "Sorry to bother you at home. You busy?"

"Just about to sit down to dinner with the missus. What can I do for you?"

"I've been going through your files, and I have a question. Most casinos use outside agencies to hire their entertainers—at least that's what I was told when I was sniffing around for clues at the Luxor and the other luxury hotel-casinos. What do you know about the missing girls? Did they work with a booking agent or talent agency?"

"Keep reading," Pudge said. "It's in there."

"Save me some time."

"Bloodgood Booking. They hired the girls, and they were the ones who reported them missing."

"Have you interviewed anyone at Bloodgood yet?"

"No. If you'll remember, I was taken off the case."

"I'm putting you back on."

"You gonna pay my salary and benefits, too?"

"Sure. I'll give you half of everything I get."

"Half of nothing's still nothing."

"Look," John said, "I can't get back to Vegas anytime soon. The captain has me on a short leash. If you can just snoop around a little. Maybe in your off hours."

Pudge laughed into the phone. "No need to twist my arm, O'Meara. I'll do what I can and get back to you."

"Great. If you can, find out how they were employed at Dracula's Castle. Were they working Vladimir's show or the bar or what? From your notes, it doesn't look like the folks at Dracula's Castle were very specific. The girls were just labeled 'entertainers.' When I went there inquiring about Payton, nobody said 'boo' about any missing girls. They were more interested in giving me a tour of the place."

"That's rich," Pudge said. "You're looking for your missing sister, and they're wooing you, as if you're Mr. Moneybags. I'm not surprised they didn't volunteer any information. The response from the people in human resources has been to be tight-lipped about the whole thing. My guess is they're being coached by upper management."

"Bloodgood might be in a position to be more candid."

"Maybe. I'll let you know what I find out."

"Thanks, Pudge. I owe you one."

"I'm sure you'll find a way to pay me back."

John hung up with Pudge and closed the file for the night. He was glad to have someone like Pudge helping him in Vegas, but he wasn't sure how long he'd be able to take being a detective by proxy. Every day he was stuck in New Orleans put more distance between him and his sister's trail, assuming she'd left one. If she was in trouble, he was running out of time.

Meanwhile, Jenny still had her eyes glued to the TV's flickering images.

John got up from the kitchen table and joined her at the futon.

"Therapy, huh?" he said and gently massaged her shoulders, which felt tense in his hands. "You'd be better off stuck on I-10 during rush-hour traffic. Or standing in line at a grocery store with an old lady ahead of you digging for change in her purse and a baby one aisle over screaming bloody hell."

Jenny reached for the remote and pushed pause, freezing the frame midmurder. She turned to face John, half of her face hidden in the shadows. "You don't need to worry about me," she whispered. "I'm gonna be okay."

"What about her?" John asked and nodded to the woman about to be diced into bits on the TV screen.

Jenny shrugged her shoulders. "She's toast."

CHAPTER 9

JOHN SHOOK HIS head in disbelief. If Pudge was being kept at arm's length by his superiors, the rest of Vegas was clueless. The Wednesday morning edition of the *Las Vegas Sun* had scant information on the investigation going on outside city limits. In fact, just one of the bodies found—the freshest of the five excavated—was mentioned, and the paper quoted Chief Lowman as saying the body most likely belonged to a "wayward hiker" who had "perished in the heat."

Wait until Ramirez sinks her teeth into this, John mused. He didn't know the reporter, but he knew from her clips that she'd make short work of the official story.

"O'Meara!"

John looked up from his computer and saw Captain Whiting calling from his office doorway.

"What?"

The captain waved him in and then disappeared inside.

John got up uneasily from his desk. The grim look on his captain's face meant one of two things: bad news or another lecture. He pushed his chair in and made his way to Captain Whiting's office, ignoring Billy Thune and the others, who were razzing him, as if he'd just been called into the principal's office.

"All right, Jimmy," he said as soon as he reached the doorway. "Lay it on me."

"Close the door," Captain Whiting said hoarsely.

John did as he was told and then took a seat across from the captain. "You got news?"

"No, that's why I called you in. I've got nothing so far." He pointed to the online edition of the *Las Vegas Sun* on his computer screen—the same article that John had been reading. "Sounds like your friends at the LVPD are very busy this morning."

"Uh-huh," John said, playing dumb. "So how long do you want me to wait around while my sister's trail goes completely cold?"

Captain Whiting ignored the question. "What have you found out on your end?"

"What do you mean?"

"Come on. Don't tell me you've been spending all that time at your desk rearranging your files. You've been skulking around since you got back. You must have something by now."

"I've been calling her cell number and her apartment every hour. Her cell's turned off, and her apartment phone goes straight to voice mail."

"What about e-mail?"

"Her IP address shows she hasn't logged on in weeks. Her e-mail isn't being forwarded or intercepted."

"Apartment manager?"

"Hasn't seen her. But her bills are all paid up, including next month's rent and utilities."

"Neighbors?"

"Nobody knows her."

"What about friends back home? Teachers back in New York?"

"Nobody's heard from her."

"You figured this all out from your desk?"

John nodded.

The captain smiled smugly. "I've told you a million times you don't need to spend so much time beating the pavement. If you've got a phone and a computer, you can go anywhere."

"You know I don't like working here. Too stuffy."

"Yeah, I know. It's not your style, John. Not your modus operandi."

Another Whiting-ism.

"How long am I grounded?" John asked, refusing his boss's dodge.

"You're going to sit tight for at least a few more days. I can't have you out there causing trouble. From the sounds of it, Las Vegas has its hands full, but I know you're itching to get moving. If it was my sister, I would be, too. I tell you what—if we're still staring at each other by Friday, I won't tell you how to spend your weekend. But I will ask that you leave your gun at home."

John was surprised at the concession. Maybe the captain was reading the LVPD the way he was. If and when they got around to actually looking for Payton, she'd be wearing a toe tag.

But it was only Wednesday. A lot could happen by the time Friday rolled around.

"Who do you got working for you over there?"

Another surprise from the boss. The old man was always one step ahead of his detectives.

"A pencil pusher. He was demoted from a missing girls' case when he got too nosy."

"Good. What's he say?"

"I was just about to call him."

The captain frowned and then fidgeted while neither spoke. Finally, he gestured at the door and said, "Well, don't let me stop you."

John was barely at his desk when he had Pudge on the line.

"I'm stopping by Bloodgood on my way home around seven o'clock your time," Pudge said. "Hopefully, I'll have something for you before your head hits the pillow."

~~~

Pudge Feineman left for the elevator with a skip in his step. It had only been a few hours since he'd gotten off the phone with O'Meara, but he already had important information to report back to the detective. Sure, he'd had to ask his wife to hold dinner for him, but eating her wonderful cooking an hour later than normal was a small price to pay. So was working for free. He was surprised that the idea had never occurred to him before, but suddenly, he was hell bent on solving the missing girls' case *off the clock*. If he somehow cracked the thing open, despite being torn away from it prematurely, Chief Lowman would come off looking like the goat, and he'd be tagged the hero. He'd grant his first in-depth interview to Ramirez. See his mug in the papers. Maybe he'd get promoted. Shoot, maybe he'd run for office.

As for Bloodgood Booking, he couldn't wait to give O'Meara the lowdown on the place, which was hidden in a basement office in the warehouse district—and sure as hell lived up to its name. Its owner was one part Hollywood, two parts creepy. So was this never-ending corridor with low ceilings and half-burned-out fluorescent lights blinking on and off like strobe lights on amphetamines for that matter.

He turned the last corner to the elevators and was surprised to see a woman waiting alone in front of the elevator. *Where'd she come from?* Decked out in a graceful black halter dress and matching high heels, she was dressed to kill. She was standing with her back to him, but her posterior alone screamed first class. If she was representative of the kind of clientele booked by Bloodgood, the agency would never be short of happy customers. Her sweet-scented perfume choked out the basement's claustrophobic air like gardenias blooming en masse on a stiflingly hot summer night, and her blue-black bob evoked an era long gone, when women were ladies and men were gentleman. Pudge was a happily married man, and he had been for nearly twenty years. But this was one lady who could convince him to throw it all away in a heartbeat. And he hadn't even seen her face. Just her long, elegant neck. Her bare arms and shoulders as white as porcelain. Her svelte figure, alluring and nearly ghostly. She was untouchable.

"Hello, officer," she said as soon as he joined her in front of the elevator. She turned just enough to give him a glimpse of her stunning face.

"Evening," he stuttered.

They stood in awkward silence as they waited for the elevator, which could be heard clanking to a stop a few floors up.

"Are you an entertainer?" Pudge asked.

"Something like that," she said and gazed upward toward the ceiling just a foot or so away.

"Stupid question," Pudge mumbled below his breath. He hadn't felt this out of his depth since he first courted his wife in high school. Back then, he had felt butterflies in his stomach. Now, he felt something darker.

She turned then and exposed her drop-dead gorgeous eyes, eyes that could have belonged to a movie star from the old days. Pudge felt his heart in his throat.

"And you?" she asked just above a whisper. "You've come to be entertained?"

Pudge opened his mouth to answer but stuttered instead.

"You look handsome in your uniform," she purred. "I bet your wife glows with pride every time you come home from work looking like her knight in shining armor, but I suppose she worries, too."

"Worries?"

"Shouldn't she?"

She took a step closer, close enough for her perfume to make him dizzy, and Pudge felt a sickening sensation, as if the ceiling was creeping downward and the walls were inching closer.

"She worries," she said, "that her knight in shining armor won't come home one day. She worries every day that *this* day will be his last. She worries about drug dealers and gangbangers and crooked cops and two-faced politicians. She worries that her knight will be sacrificed on the altar of expediency or incompetence or politics. She worries about budget cuts and double crosses and equipment failure and moral lapses." Her breath fluttered on his face. "She worries about little things and big things, heartburn and heart attacks, until she sees nothing but blood—in your mouth, in your side." She paused to run her hand along his side from his holster to his midriff. "She sees it running like a river from your neck."

"I—"

The elevator clattered again, its pulleys whirring in the corridor, and finally, it creaked to a stop.

Pudge let his eyes drift from the bewitching siren at his side to the elevator doors in front of them.

Come on. Open.

Finally, a sliver of light appeared between them.

He felt a sigh of relief. His shirt, he suddenly realized, was bathed in sweat.

The doors creaked open and revealed a silver-haired janitor leaning over a cart, which was stuffed full of cleaners and piled high with linens.

"Sorry," the old man said. "No room."

Pudge stared back at the old man in disbelief. His stomach sank as the doors slowly crawled shut, and the elevator continued noisily downward to the subterranean parking garage beneath them.

"Poor thing," he heard the woman beside him say. "You almost made it."

He felt a quickening sensation in his ears, and suddenly, he was on his back, his glasses skidding away from him into the dark and his head recoiling as it snapped against the concrete floor. He bit his tongue and groaned. He could taste blood in his mouth, but he could see only the blurry image of the woman straddling him.

She was moaning and writhing on top of him, mumbling incoherently about the pain in her head. "Sweet Jesus," she kept saying. "Make it stop."

Finally, she pulled him up by his lapels into a sitting position, her face inches from him and her pelvis still grinding away at his. She looked ashen like someone about to lose her lunch, but when her head jerked back and her eyes grew hoods, he knew what he was looking at.

"You're one of them," he said. "I should have known."

"And you're too goddamned nosy, Dick," she said. "You should have stayed put at your desk." She brought her mouth to his and licked at the blood trickling from his lip. "You taste like fear."

"How would you know?" Pudge said, desperately trying to buy himself some time. "You're not human."

She feigned a hurt look. "Ouch."

Pudge listened for the elevator. *Get your cart off the elevator, old man!* It was his only hope.

She jerked him to his feet. "Let's take a walk."

"I don't feel like walking."

"Whatever," she hissed and stabbed a closed fist into his abdomen.

The blow doubled him over, and before he could recover, he was being dragged on his heels around the corner into the basement corridor's black depths. He could hear the elevator opening just as his face met a cement post.

"Don't make a mess," he heard someone nearby say.

"Leave me be!" she screeched.

Pudge tried to mumble something but could only choke on his teeth. He felt a crushing sensation as she tore into his jugular, followed by a delirious, sticky river of confusion. He was already too weak to struggle, too disoriented to gather for one last stand.

O'Meara! I've got to get to O'Meara! He needs to know—

The musty hallway suddenly brightened, and he could see his mother cradling him.

"Mommy?"

"Shush," she whispered and rocked him gently. "It's almost finished."

Chapter 10

She was staring at him from across the club, her blue-black bob shimmering in the incandescent light. The house music pounded in his ears, but he swore he could hear her whispering to him.

Now they stood beneath a giant sycamore, its shade blocking out the afternoon sun. Her voice was the cool breeze on his skin, the leaves gently rustling in the dappled sunlight.

I'm dreaming, he reminded himself.

No, she said without opening her mouth. *This is real. Everything else is a dream.*

She took his hand in hers and brought it to her breast, and he felt the ground beneath him give way.

This is real. This right here.

He looked down and saw nothing. Only black space at his feet. And then the ocean, blood red in the setting sun, rose up to swallow him. He tried to jerk his head above the water, tried to catch a glimpse of the sea raging around him, but the horizon in every direction was nothing but heaving waves.

I can't swim.

Let me teach you.

Who are you?

You know me. We've been together since the beginning.

The beginning of what?

Something shrill cut through the murky dream. It felt like a fist, closed fast around his shirt, pulling him through a brick wall.

What's that sound? he asked.

I don't hear it.

That! There! Something's ringing.

I don't hear it.

"John."

I don't hear it.

"John, wake up."

John shook himself awake and saw Jenny's silhouette as she lay beside him in the early morning stillness.

The phone was ringing.

"Are you going to answer that?"

"Yeah," he said and rolled over toward his nightstand. He jerked the cordless phone from its cradle. "Hello?"

"Is this Detective O'Meara?"

"Who's this?"

"Angela Ramirez with the *Las Vegas Sun*."

John sat up. The fog of sleep was slowly lifting. "Pudge gave you my number."

"Officer Feineman is dead."

John felt a burning in his temples. He glanced at his alarm clock. It was 7:30 AM, which meant it was still dark in Vegas. "When?" he asked and rubbed feverishly at his forehead. "Where?"

"The details are still sketchy, but Chief Lowman is telling reporters he was attacked last night by a wild animal at a rest stop outside of town."

"Bullshit. He was at the warehouse district checking out Bloodgood Booking."

"I know. He called me after he spoke with you. Said he was going fishing. For clues. They found him in some woods a few hundred feet from a rest stop. He wasn't buried like the others were. Just tossed into the sage brush."

"So you know about the others?"

The reporter's voice stiffened. "Of course. Lowman is running damage control, not a legitimate investigation."

"What's he got to hide?"

"I don't know, but I've got a hunch Pudge knew more than he was supposed to." She paused a moment. "Detective, Pudge told me about your missing sister. He said you think she might be mixed up in all of this. I'd like to help if I can. Maybe we can compare notes."

"Maybe."

"How soon can you be here?"

John felt his jaw harden. "I'll be on the next flight out." He didn't care if Whiting fired him or not. He had to get to Las Vegas."

"Detective?"

"Yeah?"

"Watch yourself. I'm sure whoever killed Pudge knows all about you."

John hung up the phone and rolled over to see Jenny staring at him, her head propped up on her elbow.

"Who was that?"

"A reporter in Vegas."

"It sounded serious."

"It is."

His mind raced. Pudge was dead, and he was at least partially to blame. If he hadn't sent him snooping around Bloodgood Booking, maybe he'd still be alive.

Jenny's voiced dropped to a whisper. "You're going back, aren't you?"

He nodded.

She drew closer to him, tracing her free hand along his bare chest. "You promised you'd tell me about your family sometime."

"It's … complicated," John said impatiently. He wanted to bolt, but he could sense Jenny needed connection. That, and she was waiting for an explanation. He tried to put it into the simplest terms possible, ones that wouldn't need elaboration. "My sister is on a teaching sabbatical in Vegas. Long story. But she's been missing for over two weeks. I've been trying to track her down, but so far, I've come up empty. The police in Las Vegas aren't helping. Neither is my boss."

The thought filled him with angry resolve, and he rolled out of bed, determined to make Pudge's death mean something.

"Where are you going?"

"Gotta get moving," he said and hurriedly pulled on a pair of jeans. "Gotta talk to the captain."

As he pushed his head through a plain black T-shirt, the telephone rang again.

"Now what?"

Jenny answered. "Hello?" She looked up at John and threw him a suspicious gaze. "Just a moment." She handed him the phone. "It's for you."

He took the phone, bracing for the worst. "O'Meara," he said.

"Detective, this is Cynthia Knudson over at Big Brothers Big Sisters. Just wanted to remind you about your afternoon appointment with Jason."

Ms. Knudson's voice sounded a tad lower than normal and a little froggy.

"It's awfully early," John said. "You calling from home?"

"I am. I wanted to make sure I got a hold of you before you left for work, seeing as how you're rarely reachable at the department."

"I appreciate your dedication," John said, "but now's not a good time."

"It never is with you, detective. That's why I spoke with Captain Whiting yesterday. He assured me you'd have the afternoon free. The wake-up call was his suggestion."

John felt his blood boil. Everyone was conspiring to keep him in New Orleans. "Fine. I'll see Jason on the blacktop."

"Another game of pick-up then?"

"That's what we do," John said, bristling at her condescension. "You got a problem with that?"

"Not at all, detective. I'm sure the exercise will do you good."

~~~

Her last meal, a pale-skinned girl bone dry and stone cold, was still staring back at her, maybe hoping Sadie would choke on the type A smoothie she'd just sucked down.

"Shut those eyes," Sadie said and got up from her bed to run her hands over the girl's face. "There. Now maybe I can get some goddamned sleep."

She climbed back on top of her bed and sat with her legs crossed and her head and neck reclining against a stack of pillows. With the blinds closed tight and the AC purring quietly in every room, Sadie was living in the perfect coffin. Maybe Vegas was waking up outside, but here, holed up in her three-room adobe bungalow on the city's edge, she was praying for sleep, the kind that came as the anesthesiologist walked his patient backward from one hundred to one.

Ninety-nine. Ninety-eight. Ninety-seven.

The girl, twenty-something and unlucky enough to have been dancing at Sadie's favorite nightclub only hours earlier, was sprawled against the far wall, looking so frail a light breeze might blow her over.

Sadie had nothing against her—or any of the other people she needed to feed the emptiness inside her. Some, like the leering cavemen at the gentlemen's club, deserved what they got. But most—

Ninety-six. Ninety-five. Ninety-four.

She let the thought go. She had been young once, too. She could still remember what life looked like, when the horizon went on forever, when the future could be anything. Back then, her faith in possibility, unbounded and immeasurable, met head on with the impatience of youth. The resulting cognitive dissonance tied her in knots, and she spent the better part of her early twenties trying to find a neat way to both hurry toward and delay the future.

What now?

She had no hope. No fallback plan. Just the moment. For she had become someone else, someone whose trajectory boiled down to biology, not idealism. She could believe in herself. She could try to change the world. But at the end of the day, she just needed to eat. And eating was a zero-sum game. She won. Somebody else lost.

Early on, that kind of power—*life-taking* power—had gone down like a spicy bottle of Chianti, full-bodied and intoxicating to the last drop. But nobody drank forever. Eventually, even drunkards had to wake up in the morning. Existential hole for a wicked hangover—she would have made the trade in a New York minute. Sure, she could still lose herself in the moment, but the moment—if it lasted even a few minutes—always knuckled under to the heartburn. She was beyond guilt, beyond despair. All that was left was desperation. Because she knew instinctively that if she waited too much longer, she'd end up like Vladimir: bloated and self-important and a total sellout, a fat Elvis with pointy teeth.

How could a vampire make good in Vegas?

Ninety-three. Ninety-two. Ninety-one.

~~~

John took a chest pass from Jason and grimaced. "Overkill much? I'm only ten feet away."

Jason glowered at him from the top of the key. His closely shorn afro was glistening in the sun, perspiration pouring freely from his dark brown skin. "You're not even trying, man."

"What do you mean? I just sank one from three-point land."

"Pure luck. We've been playing for an hour, and you ain't sweatin'. You're letting me beat you. Pathetic."

"You always beat me," John said and drove down the right side of the lane.

Jason turned him outside, closing him off from an easy shot. "Not like this," he panted. "Usually, you put up a decent fight. You ain't even trying."

John faked inside again and then pulled up for an uncontested jumper, draining one from sixteen feet out. "There!" he said. "Nothing but net."

Jason walked the ball to the top of the key again, but this time he held onto it. "What is it? Work? Women?"

For a seventeen-year-old, the kid was awfully smart.

"Give me the ball," John said. "I'm supposed to be mentoring you, remember?"

Another hard toss to the midsection.

John took the pass and drove to his left this time. Maybe he was distracted. Maybe he wasn't giving his best effort. But he didn't need a lecture from a high school senior. He went to his weak hand and tried a left-handed running hook, but Jason swatted it away.

"Don't go there with that weak-ass shit, man!" Jason said, pumping his fist.

John watched the basketball bounce off the asphalt and out of bounds. "Let's take a break," he said and followed the ball to the grass, where his duffel bag rested in the sun.

Jason followed, and the two paused to drink, the old man from a scuffed up water bottle, the kid from a 32-ounce bottle of an electrolyte sports drink.

John had spent the morning chewing away at Captain Whiting to let him catch the next flight to Vegas but to no avail. The captain had held firm, insisting they give the LVPD until tomorrow, Friday, to get their shit together, especially now that they'd lost one of their own. Pudge's death was a complication, not a reason to go off half-cocked. "What about

Payton?" John had growled. "You just want me to sit here and stew while she's who the hell knows where?" The question had no answer, and Captain Whiting hadn't even tried to fake his way to one.

A car backfired a block away, and John was jolted back to the present.

"Look at you, man," Jason said. "You're so juiced up you're ready to go nuclear."

John looked down at his hands. They were trembling.

"It's my sister. She's missing."

"The one who went to Vegas?"

John glared at Jason. "Yes, that one. I only have one sister, for Christ's sake."

Jason jerked his chin back and frowned. "How the hell was I supposed to know? You never talk about yourself. For all I know, you got a hundred sisters and seventy-three-and-a-half brothers."

"Sorry."

Jason dropped his gaze to the grass. Finally, he broke the silence. "Question."

"Hit me."

"If your sister's in trouble, man, what are you doing here playing hoops with me?"

~~~

John pulled into his apartment complex, hurriedly shut off the engine, and jogged up the stairs to his second-floor apartment. Sometimes, it took the wisdom of a seventeen-year-old kid to put things into perspective. If Payton was in trouble, what the hell was he doing here? Going against Captain Whiting on this one could cost him his job and going against the LVPD could land him in jail. But Payton was missing. End of discussion. His gut, as usual, told him to shoot now, ask questions later.

He stepped inside and heard Jenny in the bedroom. Now there was another kid who had something to teach him. Something about her put him immediately at ease. She was young, but she was an old soul. Spontaneous but steady. Affectionate without being too clingy. And to think she'd been only inches away from being sacrificed by a bunch of voodoo hacks. Their god's loss was the detective's gain.

"Hey, sweetheart," he said and pushed the bedroom door open. "I'm sorry to bug out on you again, but I need to catch a—"

Someone—not Jenny—was hunched over John's dresser and rummaging through his things.

In one fluid motion, the intruder yanked the top drawer free, pivoted, and hurled it at John.

John dodged the drawer and its contents and jerked his sidearm free. He fired. The guy screamed and clutched his right arm. Blood spurted between his fingers as he fell to his knees. In two long strides, John reached him and aimed his pistol at his forehead.

"Who are you?" John demanded.

The burly thug, a Caucasian male about forty-five years old but in awesome shape, slowly raised his head. He had the face of a bouncer and the scars to prove it—two above his right eye and one that cut right through his lower lip.

"You got me, detective."

John felt no popping sensation in his ears, which told him the man was human—and not like the crazed stripper back at Dracula's Castle. He eased his finger off the trigger but kept his weapon aimed at the intruder's face. "Who sent you, asshole?"

"Sweety, I'm home."

Jenny.

John kept his eyes on the brute. "Move an inch, and I'm spraying your brains all over that wall behind you." He called out to his girlfriend in the entryway, "Jenny, call the police!"

"What?" she asked. "Why?"

"Do it!" John barked.

"Okay, okay," she said. The quiver in her voice told John she suddenly understood the gravity of the situation.

Before she could leave, someone else joined the conversation.

"Well, well, well, what do we got here? Stop gawking, honey, and get your pretty little ass inside."

John heard the door slam shut and the deadbolt being secured. He kept his eyes on the bruiser, who was smirking now.

"We got company, Apollo."

"No shit, T-Bone," the man out in the entryway said. "I just landed me a live one. Can we keep her for the ride back? We got to have something to do for the next fourteen hours."

"Not out there, numb nuts. In here! Stay put, dipshit, or I'm buying a bullet in the forehead."

"Who you callin' a dipshit?"

"You want me to spell it out for you?"

"What? You think I can't spell?"

T-Bone rolled his eyes. "You see what I'm working with here?" he said to John. "It's not my fault if someone gets killed." He glanced past John and out the doorway behind him. "Apollo. Our cop friend is in here. Right now. With a gun pointed at my head. Capeesh?"

"Well, fuck a duck," Apollo called back. "Two can play that game."

John heard Jenny squeal out in pain.

"You tell Mister Cop to put his gun down or I blow a hole in the pretty little girl's head!"

T-Bone shrugged his shoulders. "You heard the man. If you want your girlfriend to walk out of here, you better give that gun of yours a rest."

John felt a giddy sensation in his gut. *Here we go.*

"Tell me who sent you," he said, ignoring T-Bone's ultimatum. "Tell me something useful before I kill you."

T-Bone laughed. "I don't think you fully appreciate the

situation here, detective. Your girl's gonna be in a world of hurt if you don't back off. Now drop the gun."

John shoved T-Bone down and turned so he could face the door. The goon had Jenny by the hair, but that wasn't what was sending shivers down John's spine. Bald head, olive skin, a body like the Hulk's—it was the bouncer from Dracula's Castle! The same joker who had tried to protect the monster-girl after she'd gone all vampy in the VIP room!

Before John could fully digest the information, he sensed T-Bone coming at him in his peripheral vision. He whirled and dropped the thug with two bullets to the forehead, but as quickly as he'd handled T-Bone, Apollo had lumbered the ten paces between them and was on top of him, choking him from behind with his forearm.

"You killed my friend!" Apollo spat, his mouth less than an inch from John's ear. "Now I'm gonna kill you."

John tried to call to Jenny, to tell her to get out, but he couldn't breathe, much less talk. He knew from previous experience what it felt like to pass out, and the blinking stars closing in around his vision told him he was about to take a good long tour of never-never land.

"Goddamn!" Apollo grunted as Jenny brought what sounded like John's prized cast-iron skillet down on his head.

Thanks for the Christmas present, Payton. I owe you one.

As he crumpled to the floor, John caught sight of Jenny slamming against the wall, the recipient of a rough toss from Apollo. He turned to face the thug and barely had time to duck as Apollo emptied his pistol into the wall above him. The bruiser was Herculean-strong, true, but a lousy shot.

Apollo pocketed his empty gun and hoisted a bar stool from beneath the kitchen counter, no doubt with the intent of scrambling John's brains with it.

John fired twice, splintering the doorjamb just above Apollo's head with one round, but he missed both times. He never got off a third shot. The bar stool hit him square in the face, and the last thing he saw was Apollo dragging Jenny by the hair through the front door.

"I'll see you again, cop!"

John tried to cough out a response, but nothing came. Was he hearing sirens? The walls were closing in.

Chapter 11

John came to with Captain Whiting's bald mug in his face.

"You did it again, O'Meara. I'm impressed."

The detective fought off a disorienting wave of nausea. "Where am I?" he asked and then recognized his apartment's entryway, his nose only a couple inches from the tile floor. He sat up and leaned against the wall. "Where's Jenny?"

"Jenny who?"

"The girl we saved from being sacrificed last week."

"What? What was she doing here?"

John wiped a streak of caked blood from his lips. "She didn't want to go back to her apartment the night I took her home," he said, not bothering to couch the truth in something more palatable, "so she stayed with me."

"You mean to tell me you've been shacking up with a victim? Is she a minor?"

John glared at his boss. "I only break one cardinal rule at a time, captain. She's twenty-five."

Captain Whiting, who had been kneeling beside John, retook his feet and stood quietly a moment, surveying the crime scene. He nodded to the carnage in the bedroom. "I suppose this gentleman is our only witness," he said hoarsely.

John glanced past the captain and spotted T-Bone's dead

body, his legs splayed awkwardly and his cowboy boots pointing north. "Yup. There's your witness. Too bad he can't talk."

"Too bad."

"Look, captain—"

"Save it, detective. As of right now, you're suspended from the department. Once we get this sorted out, I'll decide on disciplinary actions. In the meantime, you're going to have to give a statement, so why don't you practice on me? What happened?"

John paused to gather his thoughts. "It happened pretty fast. I was coming home after shooting hoops with Jason. Thought I heard Jenny in the bedroom. Turns out it was our friend there. His accomplice called him T-Bone."

"Accomplice? There was more than one?"

"Uh-huh. A bouncer by the name of Apollo. Showed up while I was interrogating T-Bone. I've seen him before. At Dracula's Castle. He's got Jenny."

"Christ," the captain said, "this is gonna get messy."

"You sure you wanna suspend me?"

Captain Whiting ignored the question. "I'll need a physical description of this Apollo fellow."

John nodded. "Mediterranean. Midtwenties. Burly. Shaved quaff. Not much between the ears."

The captain cocked his head in amusement. "*Mediterranean?*"

"Right. I'm not sure what race he belongs to. Could be Italian—or Moroccan—for all I know. Hell, he could be part Hispanic."

"A mongrel, maybe."

"I wouldn't say that to his face. He'll bite it off."

"He's that tough?"

"Quick, too."

"Accent?"

"No, as far as I can tell he's homegrown."

Captain Whiting helped John to his feet and then hollered to Billy Thune, waving him over.

"Detective Thune," he said as soon as Billy joined them in the entryway, "one of our assailants is still on the loose—and armed. Worse, he's got a hostage with him. O'Meara here is going to give you a description of the suspect and the hostage. As soon as he's finished, I want you to send a bulletin to every officer and state trooper within city limits."

"Apollo will be hoofin' it back to Vegas," John interrupted.

Captain Whiting turned to John. "Are you sure about that?"

"Positive. He's somebody else's pawn. He'll be going back to show off his trophy."

"Well, that narrows it down to five major highways and God knows how many back roads and goat trails."

"Shut 'em all down," John said.

"We'll do the best we can," the captain said. "But you know we don't have time or the manpower to set up roadblocks on every route out of here. Our suspect already has a healthy head start. More to the point, we don't even know what kind of vehicle we're tracking or if it's got Nevada plates. And you can't even identify the suspect's race. Do you really want me to turn the whole force loose looking for a large brown man with a white woman in a car?"

"Olive-skinned," John protested. "Not brown. I told you. He's either North African or Italian or maybe Hispanic or of mixed race."

"Exactly," the captain said, waving his hand in a gesture of futility. "I'm not going to declare open season on all interracial couples leaving New Orleans!"

Thune, an African-American, stifled a laugh. "Don't worry, captain. I'll take it from here."

"Fine, detective," Captain Whiting said and then stopped himself. "One more thing, O'Meara. Be sure to take your cell phone with you … in case we need to reach you while you're gone."

John studied the captain's eyes, but his boss was showing his best poker face. "Are you saying what I think you're saying?"

"I don't know what you're talking about, detective. You're suspended from the department on paid leave. As far as I know, you'll be staying with family while your apartment remains a crime scene."

"Payton's my only family."

"That's correct," the captain said, still straight-faced.

"What about our friends in blue in Vegas?"

"I suggest you leave a wide berth. I'll be contacting them shortly to coordinate our manhunt. Unless we nab him here in the next few minutes, Apollo will be in their backyard in a matter of hours, but I'm not counting on them to do anything other than sit on their collective hands, which as far as I can tell is the only thing the LVPD is good at."

Once again the captain was full of surprises.

"You want him taking this?" Billy interjected as he stooped to pick up John's mostly spent revolver, which had been lying on the entryway floor.

The captain assented with a worried frown. "I have a hunch he'll need it where he's going."

~~~

John arrived in Vegas just before midnight. He found a nondescript hotel near the airport, tucked safely away from the Strip, and vowed to catch a few hours of sleep. He would need to be rested and ready tomorrow. He had barely gotten comfortable on the queen-sized bed when the phone rang.

"O'Meara," he said.

"Detective, this is your captain."

"What's the news?"

Captain Whiting sighed hoarsely into the phone. "The suspect has not been spotted and is still at large. I've called off the search, although officers have been instructed to continue keeping a watchful eye for passengers that match your descriptions."

John felt his shoulders sag. He'd known the chances of catching Apollo hightailing it out of New Orleans were slim to none, but he had still held out hope that Apollo, as dense as he was, would make a mistake. "What about the LVPD?"

"Chief Lowman has assigned an officer to coordinate efforts with our precinct."

"One officer?"

"Were you expecting more?"

John unfurled a sour frown. "No."

"I'll keep you posted on any developments. In the meantime, detective, I suggest you maintain a low profile—wherever you are."

John thanked his captain for the call and hung up. As worried as he was about Jenny, he felt confident that she was safe for the moment. She would be of little use to Apollo dead. Even Apollo's employers would try to use her as a bargaining chip if they followed typical protocol, perhaps to scare John off Vladimir's trail. But none of that changed the fact that Jenny was in serious danger and most likely scared out of her wits. She was, in fact, suffering because of John, and the thought filled him with hopeless rage. He wanted to strike back at someone—anyone—but knew his hands were tied.

Jenny was his responsibility, and he would have to keep a cooler head than his enemies to save her.

~~~

John followed an elderly receptionist past several cubicles at *Las Vegas Sun* headquarters until they reached a medium-sized conference room. His ears were still ringing from yesterday's gun battle with T-Bone and Apollo, and his face felt like someone had used it to mop his kitchen floor. But he was glad to be out of bed, where sleep had felt more like work than rest, and finally doing something.

He had spent most of the night trying to get a grip on his feelings for Jenny. If anything bad happened to her—worse than being kidnapped for the second time in just over a week—he would carry the guilt with him to his grave. As it was, he knew he could no longer continue on with their romantic relationship. She needed to heal, and besides, she belonged on a therapist's couch, not in a cop's bed.

"She'll be with you in a moment," the elderly receptionist said and left for the front desk.

"Thanks," he said and took a seat at the long, rectangular conference table.

A Latino woman with long dark hair and a lovely olive-toned complexion stuck her head through the doorway a moment later. "Are you Detective O'Meara?"

"I am," John said and stood to shake her hand as she entered. "You must be Angela Ramirez."

"In the flesh," she said and smiled curtly before she closed the door behind her. "Thanks for meeting with me. I trust your flight was uneventful. By the looks of you, I'd guess you've already met Officer Feineman's attacker."

John glanced away self-consciously. He had paused only briefly this morning in front of his hotel room's bathroom mirror to study his injuries, which included a black eye and a cut lip. At the time, he hadn't given much thought to how his appearance might strike others.

"I don't think the same goons who went after me killed Pudge," he finally said and took a seat opposite Angela, who he guessed was in her early forties. He wasn't sure how much he wanted to share with the reporter. He would have to choose his words carefully. "They were ... human. One's on ice back in New Orleans."

"There was more than one?"

"Trouble usually comes in pairs." Should he tell Ramirez about Jenny? For the moment, he decided on discretion. "I need to get something straight up front."

"What's that?"

"As far as the authorities are concerned, I'm back in New Orleans. If the LVPD gets wind of me being here, I'll be too hamstrung to get anything done."

"In other words, you don't want to be quoted in the paper."

"I don't even want to be *mentioned* in the paper."

"Not to worry, detective. This meeting like any we might have in the future is strictly off the record. I routinely work with anonymous sources without ever divulging their identities. In this case, I want to find Pudge's killers, and I'm convinced they can be traced to Dracula's Castle and possibly the mayor. I'm hoping you'll be able to help me, because we're both after the same thing."

John nodded slowly. "Pudge told me a bit about your work surrounding the missing girls, and I've seen your byline in his notes; but I'll admit I don't know much about your angle. Mind filling me in?"

"I started covering this story six months ago after an exotic dancer at the gentlemen's club at Dracula's Castle disappeared. She was the first of several to go missing. When an intern at the mayor's office went missing, I started exploring a possible connection."

"Which is?"

"Mayor Ward is an old college chum of the owner, Alistair Bishop. The mayor fast-tracked the construction permits for Dracula's Castle, which was opposed by several business leaders in the chamber of commerce who were concerned about its adult-oriented theme. In recent years, Las Vegas has been trying to remake itself into a more family-friendly tourist destination. Dracula's Castle bucked that trend, and it would have never been built without the mayor's behind-the-scenes endorsement."

"What about this Alistair Bishop character? Could he be involved?"

"Not likely. He's an eccentric businessman, an East Coaster who came to Vegas to spend some of his money opening Dracula's Castle, which is his pet project, sort of a lifelong fantasy. But my guess is he's harmless. His only fault is in the company he keeps."

"The mayor."

"Right. Mayor Ward is about to be indicted for a whole host of ethics violations. Most of the allegations are over a year old and involve bribery, kickbacks—that kind of stuff. But the most recent—that he's having or has had more than one extramarital affair—puts him on the hot seat. Conveniently enough for him, the intern who was going to come forward with the details disappeared."

"Tina Porter."

"You got it. That's when I started wondering if there was a connection between her disappearance and the other missing girls'. Admittedly, it's a stretch, but it's possible the mayor has played a role in each."

"Interesting. So you think Vladimir is just a cog in the machine, and that someone else, the mayor, is pulling his strings."

John wondered if his honor was connected with Payton's disappearance, too. If so, he would see to it that the illustrious mayor never had a moment's peace as long as he lived.

"What about Chief Lowman? Pudge claimed he was demoted because he was asking too many questions about the missing girls. Could the chief be involved?"

"I'm not so sure. Chief Lowman has his faults, but I have a hard time believing he would be involved with missing girls and … vampires."

"So you've seen one of them?"

"No, but I've seen Vladimir's act, and I tell you, it's real."

John shook his head in wonderment. "It's definitely *surreal*. What about Pudge?"

"I think he was right to trace everything back to Dracula's

Castle, but I'm not convinced he was fired as part of a cover up. He's botched other high-level cases in the past usually because of sloppy work—not adhering to procedure while procuring warrants and that kind of stuff. It's possible Chief Lowman didn't want him tainting this case."

John frowned. It seemed more likely that Pudge was on track and had been derailed. "So far, I've gotten no help from the LVPD with my missing sister. I sense a lot of foot dragging. Maybe Pudge was right. Maybe Lowman is working with the mayor."

The reporter nodded thoughtfully. "Anything's possible at this point. There's still so much we don't know."

All John knew was that his sister and now his girlfriend were in trouble, and if he didn't make headway soon, both might end up like Pudge. He stood up and handed Angela his card. "Thanks for your time. If you need me, you can reach me on my cell phone."

"What's your next move?"

"Lay low until this evening."

"Then what?"

"I'm hoping to catch up with Pudge's widow," he said. "Then I'm gonna go catch a show."

~~~

What did he put in my water?

Jenny squinted at the bottled water sitting next to her in the console and then gazed lazily outside, her head dipping to her chin twice as she tried to take in the city whizzing past her window, block by block.

"Where are we?" she asked, unable to stop from slurring the words.

"Vegas," Apollo said testily.

The hazy feeling in Jenny's head migrated to her heart. "Don't worry," she said, feeling sorry for her muscular captor, who looked ready to implode from the stress of driving all night. "We'll be okay."

"I'm not worried about me," Apollo said, his expression darkening as he spoke.

Jenny felt her stomach lurch, but she couldn't put the fear to words. "We'll be okay," she repeated, as if saying it was enough to make it real. "We'll be okay."

Daylight had come hours ago, but everything looked increasingly muddled. She tried hard to concentrate, to slow the world down long enough to understand it, but she found herself processing each moment after it had already gone by, not as it arrived. She could see Apollo's face darken. What had he just said?

"We'll be okay," she whispered to herself.

A dizzying, deafening blur of cars. Then silence as Apollo guided their car down a narrow alley. Once outside, he took her hand, and she held onto it, as if it had belonged to her father. She trusted the big man. He was all she had.

Musty.

A claustrophobic hallway. Then the sweet smell of cigar smoke.

Where am I?

A maze of elevators and escalators. Soulless pop music coming from somewhere above.

I feel sick.

And then noise, exploding like a wave on the surf, as the last elevator door opened. A sea of slot machines screamed from every direction. People jawed at one another and their machines in an incomprehensible jumble, and Jenny closed her eyes against the chaos.

She followed Apollo, her tiny hand gripping his, through the unrelenting noise until they had at last reached a card table, where the dealer was spitting out cards fast and furious and the players were hunkered down in stony silence, their faceless supporters crowding around them in a semicircle buzzing with energy.

"Here she is," Jenny heard Apollo say.

An elegantly dressed man turned and smiled a toothy grin. Beside him sat the most beautiful woman Jenny had ever seen. She had the face of an angel, but her eyes were vacant and soulless.

"I am finished for the moment," the elegantly dressed man said to the dealer and then returned his attention to Apollo. "You did well, my friend. Go home and get some rest before your next shift."

Jenny felt Apollo's grip loosen, and she tried to reassure him, to make eye contact and tell him they would be okay; however, he then let go, and all she could see was his broad back, a long bead of sweat splitting his gray T-shirt down the middle, as he walked away.

"Sit," the elegantly dressed man said.

Jenny looked down and saw a plush loveseat with room enough for three. The card table was now several yards away, but the cauldron of noise continued unabated.

"I—"

Her head swam. She remembered the bogus voodoo ritual that had nearly claimed her life eight days earlier. She could hear the pulsing rap music and smell the onions on the Bringer's breath, but when she opened her eyes, she saw the elegantly dressed man staring back at her.

"I don't want to do this," the beautiful woman said.

"But you hate her."

"What? I don't even know her."

"Yes, you do, my darling. And you hate her for having what you want."

"I don't know what you're talking about."

Jenny raised her hands in protest. "Stop," she pleaded. "Please, stop talking." Her ears felt like she was coming in at thirty thousand feet. "I'm okay, I'm okay, I'm okay."

She was seated now, between the elegantly dressed man and the beautiful woman. The casino's noise drifted in and drifted out, and she could see herself from above—a tiny girl seated on a sofa and surrounded by people and games and ringing machines for as far as the eye could see.

"At least make it quick," the beautiful woman said.

"Indeed not," the elegantly dressed man said. "She's to become one of us."

"Christ."

"No, darling, not even God can help her now, but I promise to be discreet."

"What? Here? Now? In front of everyone?"

"Why not? The lemmings won't see a thing. We are just three lovers enjoying a public display of affection."

Jenny felt a tingling sensation on her throat as the man traced her neck with fingernails as delicate as a woman's but as sharp as a surgeon's scalpel.

"I wanna go home," she said as a tear streaked down her cheek.

"You will, dear. You will."

~~~

Judy Feineman knelt in front of a weathered gravestone, her silhouette framed in gold by the early evening sun. She was whispering softly to herself or maybe to Pudge.

John waited until she had finished before he approached her.

"Detective O'Meara?" she asked as she struggled to her feet.

"That's me," he said and offered her his arm to steady her. "And you must be Mrs. Feineman."

"Please," she said and brushed aside her wavy brunette hair, which was blowing every which way in the warm evening breeze, "call me Judy."

She had a sweet face, complete with chubby cheeks and big brown eyes, and John could sense in her thousand-yard stare a profound, earth-shattering sense of loss. She looked shell-shocked, as if she still couldn't quite believe what had happened. John knew enough about loss to know that her world would never be the same. *She* would never be the same.

"All right," the detective said with a smile.

Judy glanced down at the gravestone at their feet. "My father died when I was seven. He was killed in the line of duty. Just like Harry." She let her gaze drift from her father's grave to the empty grass plot beside it. "I've arranged to have Harry buried next to him."

John coughed into his fist self-consciously. "I only knew your husband a short time. He was trying to help me find my missing sister when he was murdered."

"Murdered?" Judy asked without looking all that surprised.

John guided her to the cool shade of an ancient Italian cypress. She looked weak, and he wondered if she was ready for the truth.

"Did he tell you about the missing girls' case?"

She nodded yes. "He tells me everything."

"So you know about your husband being demoted to the desk?"

"I do," she said and bit her lower lip in an effort to fight off another round of tears. "I've promised myself I'll be a good girl at the burial on Monday, but God, I'd like to tell the chief to stick it where the sun don't shine."

"So you think Pudge was on to something?"

"I *know* he was," she answered, her eyes narrowing with resolve. "He told me Dracula's Castle was a deathtrap for beautiful girls and that the featured act there, some creep named Vladimir, was the one doing the killing."

"Judy," John said and then felt his throat catch. "Your husband was chasing down a lead for me when he—"

The expression on Judy's face changed from anger to deep sympathy. "Oh no you don't," she said and placed her hand gently on John's shoulder. "My husband died doing his duty. Don't go carrying around guilt that doesn't belong to you."

John laughed quietly. "You could see that about me?"

"Honey, it's written all over your face." Judy looked away and exhaled slowly from her mouth. "Do me a favor, will you, detective?" she said and then locked eyes with him. "Find the monster responsible—and give him what he gave my Harry."

Chapter 12

"Is this seat taken?" an older gentleman asked as the show was just about to get underway.

"No," John answered. He had hoped his would be a table for one, but sharing it with someone else might have made him look less conspicuous, too.

"Excellent," the man said and removed a French beret. He was dressed ostentatiously in mustard-colored silk pajamas. "I hate to watch Vladimir alone. He's damn good—but positively frightening."

"You've got that right."

"So you've seen his act before?"

"Once."

The gentleman, who was slim but looked soft, nodded in approval. "And what did you think?"

"I wasn't sure what to make of it."

"Ah, so you're here to untangle the mystery."

"Something like that." John's eyes watered from the effects of the man's cologne, which was strong enough to ward off, well, a host of vampires. "How 'bout yourself? You sound like a fan."

"Indeed," the man said. "I'm Vladimir's biggest fan. I'm

also his employer. I own this casino." He extended his hand to John. "I'm Alistair Bishop. And you are?"

"Pleased to meet you," John said, momentarily flummoxed. "I'm—My name's John."

Mr. Bishop's eyes narrowed below his balding forehead, and his thin lips crinkled into a frown. "Do you have a last name, John?"

Was the owner of Dracula's Castle a harmless eccentric like Angela had claimed? Or in on the killings? John decided to risk finding out. "O'Meara," he said. "I'm from out of town."

"Everyone in Vegas is," Mr. Bishop said without missing a beat.

John searched his face for a hint of recognition but saw none. If Mr. Bishop knew who the detective was, he was the consummate actor.

The house lights lowered.

"Well, John O'Meara, I hope you enjoy the show. Please excuse me if I'm not much of a conversationalist during Vladimir's act. I tend to lose myself in his performance."

"You're not the only one," John said and sank into his seat as the theatrics began.

The show began once again with the band of gypsies, followed by the rough-edged horsemen, who, as before, softened up the crowd nicely for Vladimir. For his part, the magician was once again the consummate showman, blending humor, illusions, and witty repartee with apparent ease. His routine included a handful of new twists but concluded the same way with the same bloody showstopper. John's attempts at separating illusion from truth bore little fruit, for Vladimir wielded an almost hypnotic control over the audience, including the detective, as he had the first time John took in his show. But John noticed that he was less disoriented during the climax. The claustrophobic sensation, felt keenly in his ears before, was still there, but it was familiar now and therefore less bewildering.

But the violence of Vladimir's act remained just as unsettling. The dynamic between performer and audience was perhaps the most disturbing mystery of all. Somehow, Vladimir convinced those watching his show to applaud death. He made them feel a part of the ritualistic killing, as if they had played an important role in a worthy goal—the murder of his beautiful assistant, this time a beautiful young redhead named Lucy. As the blood drained from her face and she turned a ghastly shade of gray, the audience held its collective breath, not in horror but in anticipation. Her death was their reward.

After Vladimir had returned with his assistant, once again very much alive, for a curtain call, John glanced out of the corner of his eye at his table companion and was surprised to find Alistair Bishop slumped in his chair, recoiling in apocalyptic fear. What could he see that the others couldn't?

~~~

"You rang?"

Vladimir looked up from his empty mirror, a towel wrapped around his neck, his dark mane glistening with sweat. "Ah, Sadie darling," he said and waved her inside. "Please. Come in."

She entered his dressing room and, without prompting, closed the door behind her. Why wait for the magician to issue another pompous request?

She moved to cover her cleavage with her slinky gown but stopped herself. Usually by now, she could feel her skin crawling halfway up her neck, but tonight, something was up. Instead of devouring her with his eyes or leering at her with that toothy grin of his, Vladimir was stifling a yawn.

"So what's so important you needed to tear me away from the club?" she asked impatiently.

He rubbed his chin thoughtfully. "I think perhaps I am bored."

Oh, God.

Sadie felt like kicking herself. She should have recognized the look on his face the moment she'd come through the door. The only time he didn't want to get in her pants was when something was wrong with the show. And the only thing that was ever wrong with the show was Vladimir. The guy had the attention span of a toddler still in diapers.

"What's wrong with Lucy?" she protested, already knowing the source of his discontent. "She's barely gotten her feet wet, and she's already every bit as good as Sasha was, who, I might add, you said you absolutely adored—right before you demoted her to the gentlemen's club."

"Oh, of course," Vladimir said and waved off the question. "Lucy is … *wonderful*. Perhaps the best assistant to ever grace the stage—aside from you, of course. But life goes on, no?"

"You've got the itch."

"Yes, and I need someone new to scratch it."

Sadie shook her head in amusement. He was a jackass, but he had his moments.

"I suppose you'll want my help finding you an extra special new toy."

"Ah, but we already have one." Vladimir's eyes narrowed as he threw Sadie a knowing look. "Ms. Jenny Cross would make a fine assistant, don't you think?"

So *that* was it. The bastard wasn't bored. He didn't have an itch that needed scratching. He had brought her to his dressing room in order to make her squirm. Again. The routine was getting old. She already regretted watching passively as he turned Jenny, and now he wanted to push the envelope further.

"What if I don't feel like playing?"

Vladimir frowned. "I do not understand. Why do you say such things?" He shook his head in disgust. "You have not been yourself lately."

"Oh? And who am I supposed to be?"

"Mine," Vladimir said as a shadow crept across his face. "To do with as I please."

Sadie opened her mouth to put the cretin in his place, but he cut her off.

"I have not forgotten your little act of rebellion the other day," he said, practically spitting out the words. "How you walked out on me. And today with our little Jenny—if I did not know better, I would think you were growing a conscience."

Sadie rolled her eyes. "I butchered the pig you were so worried about, didn't I?"

Vladimir nodded thoughtfully. "That you did, but I am afraid he is not the only policeman to have taken an interest in my work."

Sadie feigned ignorance.

"You like our friend from New Orleans," Vladimir said. "That is why you would not torture his girlfriend with me."

The magician's aim was dead center, but Sadie was not about to admit to it. "Are we done here?"

"There may come a time when I need your help again," Vladimir said. "I wonder if I can still count on you to do things properly. I wonder—" He raised his finger in triumph as a sudden realization hit him. "I know your problem, darling. You have forgotten who you are."

"Screw you. I know exactly who I am."

"Do you?" Vladimir asked and stood up from his chair, closing the distance between them. "Shall I tell you a little story?"

"Whatever."

"There was a wolf that lived in the woods near my village. I used to take long walks in the trails to soothe my soul, and I discovered this wolf one evening just after sunset. Everything was blue-gray like the sky when rain is imminent, and I was coming down from a little outcropping. Back into the dark woods beneath, there was this wolf. I practically walked on top of it. It was weak and scrawny," Vladimir said and laughed.

"It looked like a goddamned coyote, Sadie, and that is exactly what it was fighting with. I had stumbled upon an argument between this wretched wolf and this rather robust coyote, the two of them playing tug of war with some pathetic scrap of meat. A goddamned wolf, Sadie! And he was fighting for scraps with a scavenger! Why? Was he injured? Diseased? No. His problem was right here." Vladimir thumped his chest. "He did not know his place in the world, and so he suffered."

The magician brought a bony finger to Sadie's chin.

She tried to look away, but he forced her to meet his gaze.

"You are a wolf, darling. Nothing more. Nothing less."

Sadie brought her hand to his and gently but firmly removed it from her chin.

"Nice story," she said and turned to leave. "If I'm a wolf, what are you?"

She left before he could answer.

~~~

Who was she? A vampire like the stripper who had attacked him? A figment of his imagination? John had entered the gentlemen's club and looked around for the beautiful woman. He had asked the bartender about her but got no answers. So he decided to take another approach and wait in the back alley like a star-struck groupie. As John waited, he wondered if he was a fool for pinning all his hopes on the beautiful apparition he had seen at the club the night he had been attacked, but his gut told him his eyes had not deceived him. She was real, and she would surely know the thugs sent to his apartment yesterday. Finding Apollo would lead him to Jenny and maybe even to his sister.

He heard the exit door open and watched from the shadows as another stripper walked to her car, escorted like the others by a bouncer. The small parking lot was well lit beneath a pair of old-fashioned streetlamps, a nod to Alistair Bishop's fantasy in an otherwise nondescript service entrance. But a dumpster and a stack of pallets resting against the far wall offered plenty of concealment.

Another fifteen minutes went by before the door opened again, and this time, John nearly leapt out of his shoes.

Jenny.

As best as he could tell, she was unharmed. In fact, she was smiling and laughing as she was being escorted outside by none other than the bruiser who had stole her away.

John's first impulse was to reach for his gun and drop Apollo in his tracks, but he stopped himself. He didn't have a clear shot. His next inclination—to open his mouth—was just as strong, but something told him to wait.

Jenny, dressed in a black miniskirt and a revealing bikini top, hardly looked like someone in trouble. In fact, she hardly looked like herself. Her lips were smothered in scarlet, almost black lipstick, and her hips moved like they belonged to somebody else, somebody ready to gulp down the world in one bite—or maybe piss on it.

Apollo was puffing away at a stubby cigar, laughing at something Jenny had just said. He opened the door on the passenger's side of a bright yellow Mustang and then waited. Jenny, taking her time and breathing in the night air like someone who'd never smelled freedom before, was anything but the bouncer's captive. Indeed, she looked like the one in charge now, a far cry from the last time John had seen her when Apollo had been dragging her through the front door by her hair.

Should he intervene? It was now or never.

John silently slipped his gun free and unlocked the safety, but just as he was steeling himself for a confrontation with Apollo, the exit door opened again. He froze in his tracks.

There, beneath the pale light of the streetlamps, was the woman who had invaded his dreams. She was just as he remembered her—hauntingly beautiful—and she was alone.

She nodded to Apollo.

The olive-skinned muscleman shut Jenny in, careful to wait until she had situated herself, and then jogged around the yellow Mustang to enter the driver's side. "See you around, boss," he hollered back to the stunning apparition standing beside the exit.

She waved a quick good-bye, after which she closed the door to the gentlemen's club and leaned against it, looking skyward. She lingered until Apollo and Jenny were halfway down the alley and then started toward the only car left in the parking lot, a black 1960s Mercedes with tinted windows.

"Why no escort?" John asked, intercepting her before she could reach the Mercedes.

She looked up in surprise, her hair bobbing against her cheeks and her mouth forming a perfect pout. "I like trouble," she finally said. She cocked her head as she studied him. "I know you."

"We never formally met," John said. "I'm—"

"Aren't you worried you'll be found out, detective? Or do you like trouble, too?"

John looked away uncomfortably. "You have me at a disadvantage. You know my name, but I—"

"Sadie," she said, interrupting him once again. "I manage the gentlemen's club."

"*Manage?*"

She smiled an engaging smile, almost wholesome in contrast to her revealing Gothic attire, and extended her hand. "Is it so hard to imagine? A beautiful woman running the show?"

"Not at all," John said and accepted her handshake.

She wore long black velvet gloves, and her handshake was exquisitely feminine yet firm.

"It's nice to meet you ... finally. I mean—" He let the sentence trail off. He'd never before stumbled so much in front of a woman. Of course, he'd never been in the presence of someone like Sadie.

For Christ's sake, John, shut your freakin' trap before you say another word.

"Don't be embarrassed," she said. "You're in my dreams, too."

John shivered involuntarily. "What?"

"Like I said," she cooed, "I know you."

He stood with his mouth half-open, not sure what to say.

"Do you like to dance, detective?"

"God, no."

She motioned for him to get in the Mercedes. "Come on. I want to show you something."

John opened the passenger side door and climbed in. If he was going to find Payton and help Jenny, he had to play it Sadie's way—for now.

~~~

"What the hell is this place?" John asked as he and Sadie were waved past a long line of people, down a spiral staircase, and into a cramped basement discothèque.

"Be careful, detective," Sadie said and immediately began moving to the sultry beat thumping from the speakers. "You might have fun."

He followed her into the throbbing crowd, which stunk of perfume, clove cigarettes, and body odor. As he gazed at the others sweating on the dance floor in an Ecstasy-driven haze, all of them dressed in varying degrees of Gothic chic, he felt conspicuous in street clothes. At least his T-shirt was black.

"Come on," Sadie said and grabbed his hands in hers. "Loosen up. If you're not careful, you're going to die a boring old man."

There was that smile again. Sadie, dressed in what amounted to a negligee, somehow looked classy, elegant in fact. Her long eyelashes framed a stunning pair of hazel eyes, and her mouth looked imminently kissable, her lower lip practically quivering in delight.

"You're enjoying this, aren't you?"

She laughed and tossed her hair. "Aren't you?" She stopped dancing long enough to size him up and then mocked him with a pout. "Poor boy got no rhythm."

"I've got rhythm," John protested. "I just don't waste it on the dance floor."

"Oh?" she said and raised her eyebrows seductively. She took him by the hand. "Follow me."

He followed her through the crowd once again. The next thing he knew, they were outside in the alley and she had him pinned against the wall.

"What do you want from me, detective?"

"Nothing," he lied.

Her eyes, full of carefree mischief before, suddenly looked leaden with dread. She had been calling the shots, controlling every moment, since their meeting in front of her Mercedes, but now she looked like a young girl, lost and hoping for rescue.

"Kiss me," she breathed.

He closed his eyes and felt himself plunging into the same sea he'd been drowning beneath in his dreams. He had no fear. No regrets. Nothing but the moment.

"No!" she said and pried her lips free from his. "Not like this."

He wiped a trace of fresh blood from his still wounded lower lip. "What's wrong?"

She started for the street, bypassing the club altogether, and ignored the question. "I'm hungry. Let's get something to eat."

"Okay," he said and trotted to catch up.

Vegas at 4 AM, brighter than the brightest day, cut through even her Mercedes' tinted windows, and Sadie, foundering just minutes before, looked perfectly in her element as they drove down the Strip, searching for a place to grab a bite to eat. Her porcelain skin glowed blue, then white, then yellow-orange beneath the ever-changing neon display, and her French bob fluttered in the wind whistling through her window, which was cracked open a half inch.

John leaned against the passenger's side. His mood was shifting by the second from ebullient to crestfallen to numb. For the moment, he felt perfectly content, like someone with a hearty meal and two glasses of wine in his stomach.

"Who *are* you?" he asked just loud enough to be heard above the whirring engine.

"Nobody," she said.

"Bullshit."

They stopped at a crowded all-night diner and were ushered to a booth. He was surprised to learn that her appetite, ravenous just minutes earlier, had disappeared. While he ordered steak and fries, she nursed a Bloody Mary.

"Damn, that thing's spicy," he said. "I can smell the Tabasco sauce from here."

"I can barely taste it," she said quietly.

John tried to get a bead on the beautiful woman sitting across from him, but she was impossible to read. He could feel himself feeding off her elusiveness, traveling from melancholy to joy and back again in the blink of an eye.

"So tell me about yourself, detective," she said. "What do you do in your spare time?"

"I don't have any spare time," he said.

She stared vacantly at her drink and gave it a stir. "Are you religious?"

John thought of Jenny. They had entertained a similar conversation only a week earlier. "I was raised Catholic," he said, "but I'm not religious about it."

"Why not?"

"I don't know. I guess I've seen too much to believe in an all-powerful, merciful God."

"Maybe God is merciful but not all-powerful. Maybe there are other powers at play."

"Maybe."

Sadie raised an eyebrow at him and then studied him quietly. "You lost someone when you were young."

"How did you know?"

"It's written all over your soul."

"You can see my soul?"

"Sure," she said and let loose another playful smile. "Can't you see mine?"

"No," he admitted. "I don't know a thing about you."

He was tempted to lose himself in her hazel eyes, which were as otherworldly as anything he'd ever experienced at Mass as a kid, but something held him back.

"What are you afraid of, detective?"

"You," he said.

She smiled mischievously. "I don't bite."

John was still several sentences back in the conversation. How had she known about his family? He thought about Madeline and the battle with leukemia she had lost. Then he thought about his parents, killed in one fateful moment on a dangerous stretch of highway. All he had left was Payton.

Payton. His sister's name alone was enough to stir something in him, a vague impulse to do something. But what? He felt lost in a fog. He glanced at Sadie, who was staring wistfully at him. So long as she was sitting across from him, he didn't mind being lost.

"What was your childhood like?" Sadie asked.

"I don't know." As he answered, he recalled vague moments alongside vivid memories. "Typical, I guess. I spent a lot of time looking after my younger sister. We used to go to the movies a lot and hang out at the park. She was younger than me, but—"

"She was looking after you, too."

"Yeah, she always has."

"What's she doing now?"

"She's a teacher. At least she was."

"Was?"

"She's on sabbatical here in Vegas. Says she wants to take one good swing at a career in the entertainment world. She's got a lovely singing voice and a pretty smile."

The waitress retrieved John's plate, empty now save for a trace of ketchup next to where his fries had been, and Sadie ordered another Bloody Mary. The diner, packed to the gills when they had first sat down in their booth, was slowly emptying.

"Have you ever been in love, detective?"

"I'm not sure."

"You're not sure?" Sadie cocked her head in amusement. "If you don't know, then the answer is no."

"What about you?"

"Once," she said.

"What happened?"

"He took my heart and put it on a stick."

John recoiled at the imagery. "Ouch. That bad, huh?"

She looked briefly like someone about to cry but then smirked and glanced away. "It wasn't so bad. I wouldn't be who I am today had I not had that experience."

"I guess that's one way to look at it."

The two continued talking for another hour until they were the last ones in the diner. Sadie, elegant, mysterious, enchanting, had what seemed like boundless energy, and it was all John could do to keep up with the conversation. He was suffering jetlag, behind on his sleep, and felt like he had gone ten rounds in a boxing ring, but there was no way he was going to be the first one to say goodnight. In fact, if they kept talking much longer, it would be time to say good morning. But Sadie saved him the trouble.

The morning sun, only moments away from making an appearance, had begun turning the sky a pale shade of indigo outside their booth window, and the neon shell enveloping the city looked strangely luminescent, as if the light was reflecting back on itself.

"I have to go," Sadie said and made a fumbling exit after she hurriedly kissed him good-bye.

It was an abrupt ending to an otherwise perfect evening.

CHAPTER 13

JOHN WOKE UP with a splitting headache. Construction workers outside were using a jackhammer, but the noise was nothing compared to the pounding in his head. He rolled over and looked at the digital alarm clock sitting on the nightstand. It was one o'clock in the afternoon.

He pulled himself upright, disoriented. Motel rooms had the nasty habit of all looking the same. This one was no different.

He walked to the window and parted the blinds as far as he dared. The midday sun was blinding. As he closed his eyes against the light, he thought about the mystery that was Sadie. She was ... all-consuming. There was no other way to describe the effect she had on him. He could still smell her perfume on his clothes.

He left the blinds and stumbled for the bathroom. The cut on his lip looked the same in the mirror. So, too, the swollen lip. But something inside him had changed. He felt numb yet more alive than he'd ever been. He wanted nothing more than to be with her.

Yet something was wrong. Someone—
Jenny.
Her name was enough to make him choke on his own

heartbeat. What the hell was happening to him? Why hadn't he asked about her or Payton last night while he was with Sadie?

He tore off his T-shirt and boxers and stepped into the shower, but the steamy water only added to the fog instead of cleansing him. The heat gave him instant comfort like Sadie had, and he felt himself once again slipping into nothingness. Every bead of hot water tempted him to forget his name, to forget why he'd come to Vegas, to forget all responsibility. He wanted only to be—

He shut off the hot water—and only the hot water—and braced himself.

"Damn!"

He lasted all of three seconds in the bone-chilling stream and then turned off the cold water as well. As he toweled off in front of the mirror, he wondered about his predicament. It was clear Sadie had him under some kind of spell. This being Vegas and she being the gentlemen's club manger at Dracula's Castle, it seemed depressingly likely that she was and had been—. He couldn't bring himself to say the word. Not just because it sounded ludicrous despite what he knew but also because he couldn't stand the thought of Sadie being one of them. Maybe Vladimir was subhuman, and certainly the stripper who had tried to take a bite out of him was messed up, but Sadie? He couldn't let himself believe it. His heart told him that her soul was still up for grabs, that she had yet to throw her lot in with the bloodsuckers.

"Good grief," he said out loud. "Would you listen to yourself?"

It was time to get cracking, time to get back on the case. Jenny's surprise appearance outside the gentlemen's club last night had added a new wrinkle to his two-pronged investigation, but something didn't add up. Either she was no longer in trouble, or she was playing it mighty cool with

Apollo. Either way, he had to find out. He had to chase her down just like his sister.

He opened the bathroom door just in time to hear his cell phone ringing. He hurried to his nightstand and answered breathlessly, "Hello?"

"O'Meara, this is your conscience speaking."

"Afternoon, captain," John said as soon as he recognized his boss's gravelly voice. "What can you tell me?"

"A little more than I could the last time we spoke," Captain Whiting answered. "We traced your boy in the morgue to the gentlemen's club at Dracula's Castle. His name is Troy 'T-Bone' Walker. Took us a while, but we got someone from human resources to talk to us on her day off. She about had a heart attack when I told her that her head bouncer was lying prone in cold storage. Anyway, she's going to break the news to his next of kin."

"What about the press? What are you telling them so far?"

"Nothing just yet. I've got another day or so before I'll have to come out with something definitive, but obviously, we're on a short leash with them, given our recent history." The captain sighed audibly. "As usual, the problem is … complicated. It's not that we don't believe you about your friend Jenny, but there's only minimal evidence that she was ever at your place. That said, she was never at her place, either, according to her landlord. So theoretically she could have gone missing a week or more ago."

"But we know that's not true."

"*You* do. *I* have to be able to produce facts."

"I'd say stick to those," John said. "No sense in spinning this mess. You can send me packing, if you have to."

"I doubt we'll have to go to those lengths, but I'll definitely give that option serious consideration."

"Gee, thanks."

"It's the least I can do."

The longer they spoke, the more clearly John was thinking. "What about Apollo? Did you get a last name? An address?" He decided for the moment not to mention last night's sighting. Whiting might call him back to New Orleans if he knew. And that would leave too much unfinished business.

"The same lady at human resources claims no one at the club goes by that name."

"She's lying."

"I know. What have you come up with so far?"

The question made John's stomach churn. "Nothing."

The captain sounded surprised. "I thought you'd have the thing cracked wide open by now."

"I've run into a bit of a snag." That was one way to put it. It beat telling his boss that he'd been put under the spell of a bewitching vampire. Before the captain could probe for details, John switched gears. "What about the LVPD? Anything from Lowman?"

"Zip. Zero. Nada."

"How come I'm not surprised?"

"You know me," Captain Whiting said. "I'm not one given to conspiracy theories, but as far as I can tell Lowman and his crew are as crooked as the Mississippi. The chief says he's got his hands full with the press and some high profile case. My antenna could be off, but I'd say it's a safe bet he's working for somebody other than the citizens of Las Vegas."

"Don't worry, captain. I'll steer clear."

"You do that."

"Oh, and captain?"

"Yeah?"

"I've got another lead, one Pudge was chasing down before he was killed."

"Good. Just make sure you're smarter than he was."

John hung up, got dressed, and walked across the parking lot to the lobby, where there was still some stale coffee left over from breakfast. He took a seat in a sofa and picked up a copy of the morning newspaper, now several hours old. Angela Ramirez's byline just below the fold on the front page caught his attention. The mayor's indictment was official now, thanks to an announcement from the attorney general's office.

Running alongside the story was a file photo of the mayor, most likely from a convention or fundraiser, now months old, in which he was smiling unapologetically at the camera. He had a full head of hair, fine features, and a picture-perfect smile.

John turned the paper over and cocked his head in amazement at the story running above Angela's. On any other day, the mayor's indictment would have garnered top billing. But not today. Chief Lowman, finally caving into pressure from the press, was coming clean on more than one front.

So this is what's been keeping him busy, John thought.

The body found by the birdwatcher out in the desert, the chief was saying now, could likely be traced to foul play, not dehydration.

So too, four other bodies, one male and three females, had been found nearby, likely the victims of some sort of ritualistic killing or cult suicide. The male body, according to the report, belonged to a businessman from Seattle. The three women had also been ID'd. Both Angela's and Pudge's hunches had proved correct: two of the women found had been strippers at Dracula's Castle. The third? Tina Porter, the mayor's missing intern. Finding the three bodies together suddenly linked the two cases and cast a shadow over the mayor.

The mayor, who had won the last election by campaigning on his conservative values, was quoted in both stories, first denying any ethics violations and secondly denying any knowledge of or involvement in his intern's disappearance.

Right, John thought. *And I'm the Virgin Mary.*

~~~

Mayor Ward looked up from the newspaper he had been reading and saw his assistant, Sissy, staring down at him from his office doorway, her head cocked tenderly to the side, her hands on her lovely hips.

"Looks like I'm not the only one who needs to get a life," he said. "What's so important it can't wait until Monday?"

"You," she said, still staring at him fondly. "I had a hunch you'd be here today. You okay?"

Sissy, his most loyal assistant, had been with him since the beginning, and as he gazed at her now with her dimpled cheeks and her innocent eyes, big and round like a doe's, he felt only regret. She had worked for him in some capacity since his first stint with the city council, and implicit throughout her years of service had been her unquestioning, unwavering faith in him. Others had fallen by the wayside in recent weeks: advisors, donors, erstwhile champions in the media. But not Sissy.

The shape of her mouth, seemingly always in midpucker. The curve of her hips was even now enough to make him temporarily forget the tsunami about to overrun him. The way she smelled like a pear tree in bloom. She had been his first and most devoted mistress, and she remained in many ways his one, true love. If it had been possible, he would have spent the last twenty years with her, not his wife, whom he also loved, albeit in a way someone loved a faithful friend, not necessarily their lover. But Sissy, too, was married. She, too, had a family. Neither of them had been willing to pay the price of letting their relationship go public. Now, of course, such a potential scandal seemed trite compared to the humiliation trotted out on the front pages of the *Las Vegas Sun*. But hindsight, as was so often said, was 20/20.

"Randy?"

"Sorry," the mayor said and smiled at his loyal assistant. "I guess I'm a little preoccupied, but I'm okay, really. How about you? How are you holding up?"

"I'm fine," she said and straightened her hair. "Do you need anything while I'm here? If you need anything at all—"

"You'll be the first person I call," he said. He nodded to

the door behind her. "Now ... I want you to turn right around and march yourself straight home. It's Saturday for Pete's sake. Enjoy the weekend with your family. I'm only going to be here for a few more minutes anyway. I just wanted to catch up on a few things and make a few calls. Figured the press would be busy hounding the police today, and no one would be around—and I was right. Mostly."

"All right," she said, deflated. "But first thing Monday morning, I want to go over your schedule. You've got a busy week coming up. Along with the charity golf game, you've got the speech at the convention center, the visit to Children's Hospital, the opening ceremony at the new park, and the meeting with the Future Business Leaders of America."

"Sounds good," he said and faked a smile.

Sissy took his hand in his. "I still believe in you, Mr. Mayor, with all my heart."

"I know you do," he said, resisting the urge to take her in his arms. "I can't tell you how much that means to me."

She showed herself out, and the mayor leaned back in his chair.

Next week's schedule, he mused, smiling bitterly to himself. He no longer enjoyed the luxury of tomorrow, let alone next week. His personal apocalypse had arrived, and the future belonged to everyone but him.

~~~

Jenny walked up a short set of wooden stairs and found the gangly magician waiting for her at center stage. He looked different now. Smaller. And not so creepy. But as she stepped closer, she remembered the hideous gulping sound he made as he drank, and she saw a brief but blinding flash of red, accompanied by the smell of her own blood, that made her choke involuntarily.

Her head was clearer now. Apollo's cocktail had worked its way through her system—and Vladimir's, she assumed. But the further she traveled from the moment of her death, the less she knew about herself. She was fading, and somebody else was taking her place.

"So this is where the magic happens," she said sarcastically.

Vladimir shook his head and frowned. "Not another beautiful woman with a chip on her shoulder, I hope."

"No chip," Jenny said. "Just curiosity. And a little dizziness."

"Dizziness?"

"Like in a dream," she said, trying to pinpoint exactly what she was experiencing. "Like I'm seeing things for the first time, but everything's coming at me too fucking fast."

She stared up at Vladimir as he tenderly pushed aside her bangs.

"Do not fret, my beautiful young assistant. As the days go by, you will forget everything that troubles you. You are like a butterfly just escaping from her cocoon."

"You make it sound almost beautiful."

Vladimir laughed lustily. "It is, my dear. It is." He stopped to gaze out at the blinding houselights. "Do you know why you are here?"

"You need a new assistant."

"More than that, my young apprentice. I need someone to help me fill the wretched, mundane lives of the people who sit out there." He pointed to the empty chairs and tables. "The people out there look to us to save them from themselves. They lead lives of quiet desperation, of pitiful numbness. They go to work. They stare at computer screens. They go home. They watch TV. They argue with their spouses. They medicate themselves to sleep. And then they wake up and do it all over again. Day after day. Week after week. Month after month. Year after year. One anesthetizing experience after another. They need somebody—anybody—to give meaning to their deaths, because that is what they are doing: they are dying, not living. If they were alive, they would not need the Internet for a nanny or television characters for friends. They would not need to watch others live to know how to do it themselves."

Jenny shook her head. She felt like a punch-drunk pugilist, fighting to hold on to consciousness. "You're making me dizzy again."

Vladimir smiled a toothy grin. "I apologize. One day, you will learn to embrace your true nature, just as I have my own." He clasped his hands together. "In the meantime, I am going to show you the ropes, as they say. And then you are going to meet someone who will help you with your paperwork and your portfolio and everything a professional entertainer needs to make it in this crazy world."

"Okay," she said but felt herself slumping to the stage's wooden floor. She sat down and put her head between her knees. All she could see was stars.

~~~

As John drove his rental car, a four-year-old VW Golf, through the city's barren industrial sector, the air conditioner went out.

"Great," he said and pushed the button to lower the windows.

A dry, blistering wind, every bit one hundred degrees, blew against his face. Sin City felt like Dante's *Inferno*.

He double-checked his directions and then descended into a parking garage that could have passed for a bunker. This was it. Bloodgood Booking was buried beneath a depressing four-story building constructed mostly of concrete, with a smattering of small windows. Down here, in the subterranean level, it was nothing but gray cement. At least it was cool.

John took the elevator up one floor, still one shy of the ground floor, and stepped into a dimly lit basement. After navigating the dark corridor, he found the door to Bloodgood Booking, marked unceremoniously with a small business card. He raised his hand to knock but opted instead to let himself in.

Inside, a wiry little man sat behind a large desk, smoking a cigar and working the phone. There was no reception area and no attached conference room, hallway, or restrooms. This—at most a three-hundred-foot square room—was it.

The man, probably in his early sixties judging by his gray hair and receding hairline, hung up the phone and then glanced up at John over his bifocals. "You're not here for a job, I hope."

"No, I'm not."

"Good," the man said hoarsely and fought off a cough. "No offense, buddy, but I've had my share of cold calls from has-beens this week."

John flashed him his badge. "Actually, I'm looking for an up-and-comer. I'm curious if she tried out with you."

"Oh? What's this up-and-comer's name?"

"Payton Standley. She might be going by her maiden name, O'Meara." John removed his sister's photo and showed it to the booking agent.

The man's face, previously as animated as a game of bingo at the local nursing home, lit up like a Christmas tree. "Oh, yes, I remember this one. Bright gal. Classier than most. She auditioned brilliantly."

John felt his stomach leap. This man, nearsighted and billowing smoke, was the first to recognize Payton's photo. It was all he could do not to hurdle his desk and start shaking the guy by his navy blue sport jacket's lapels. He wanted whatever he could give him—now!

"And?"

"And nothing. She never showed up for work."

"What do you mean?"

"Just what I said. She won a slot on center stage but never showed up."

"How can you be so sure?"

"Simple. Everyone signs a W-2 on the first day of work. Hers is blank." The man got up from his desk and walked to a huge row of file cabinets behind him. After he rummaged through one of them for a moment, he found what he was looking for and returned with Payton's file.

John studied the W-2 form. No signature. "Why does Bloodgood Booking still have a file on my sister?"

"Your *sister*?" the man repeated and raised an eyebrow above his bifocals. "I'm Eugene Bettencourt by the way." He extended his hand. "And I know all about you, detective."

John refused the handshake. "Answer my question."

"No need to get all hot under the collar, pal. I'm not gonna go tattling on you for showing your face in town again."

"Why not?"

"There's no money in it." He eased back into his leather chair. "Besides, I've got nothing to hide. You got questions? Fire away."

"You can start by answering my last question. Why do you still have my sister's file if she never showed up for work?"

The booking agent pointed to the huge row of file cabinets behind him. "I keep everything, understand? You never know when you might need a name or a number in this business, but in your sister's case, I've got an ulterior motive."

"Which is?"

"I hope she comes back. She was special. I'll be holding onto her file for a good long while."

John didn't know what to make of the little man in front of him. Was he on the up and up? Or the usual fast-talker? He decided to take another approach. "An officer from the Las Vegas Police Department stopped by here two days ago. A Harry Feineman. Did you meet with him?"

"Now there's a name I don't recognize. Nobody from the police has been to see me, but then again, I'm not usually here. You got lucky finding me at my desk."

"How come you keep such odd hours?"

"Survival, pal. If I kept regular nine-to-five hours, I'd get nothing done. Too busy with the parade of actor and singer wannabes coming in to beg me for their first break. Understand?"

"Why don't you hire a receptionist?"

"Waste of money. I'm old school. I've been doing this since before you were wearing diapers, kid."

John pulled out Pudge's list of missing women who had worked at the casino. "What about these ladies?"

Bettencourt reviewed the list. "Oh, yeah. I know all these names. I'm the one who reported them missing. If they don't get paid, *I* don't get paid. If someone's killing my talent, they're killing my bottom line."

"What position did they hold at Dracula's Castle?"

The old man gave John a wry grin. "What do *you* think, detective?"

"Main stage, assistant to Vladimir, the magician."

"Bingo!" Bettencourt shuffled some papers on his desk. "Now, I hate to give you the bum's rush, but I've got a talent agency to run. If you need anything else, you know where to find me … some of the time."

"You got a business card?"

"Not for you, my friend. My info's on the door."

"A Web site?"

"Like I said, I'm old school. Everybody who's anybody knows where to find me."

"Okay," John said and eyed a set of fancy oversized pencils resting horizontally in a flat wooden box on the booking agent's desk. "Mind if I borrow one of those to write down your contact info outside on the door?"

"Keep it," Bettencourt said and tossed him one of the already sharpened pencils.

John caught the pencil away from his body, wary of its sharp point, and was surprised by the keepsake's substantial size and weight. "Impressive," he said as he eyed the bulky pencil. "You could stake a tent with a set of these."

"Life's too short to do anything halfway," Bettencourt

said, aiming a finger at him and pretending to shoot. "Remember, word of mouth, pal. It's the bread and butter of the entertainment industry. Everything else is just so much noise—empty hype peddled by hucksters and con artists. You're looking at the real McCoy."

~~~

John fidgeted impatiently at the elevator. Was Bettencourt on the level? He seemed like a straight shooter, but then again, that was his shtick. As someone who had built a lifelong career by shaping other people's perceptions of him, he was, beneath it all, a slick salesman, but he was the only link to Payton that John had at the moment. His recounting of the missing girls jibed with Pudge's as well as Angela's. The next step was to find someone—anyone—at Dracula's Castle who'd be willing to talk. If that failed, he would have to force Vladimir's hand somehow. Time was running out.

Finally, the elevator chimed, and the door lumbered open. A woman inside, dressed in a baby blue jogging suit, more fashion statement than functional sportswear, was just lowering her hood. She looked up at John, and as their eyes met, John felt the familiar popping in his ears.

"Jenny?"

"Hey," she said bleakly.

The sweet girl from Ponchatoula with the gorgeous smile and the all-American charisma was gone. In her place stood a washed-out, burned-out, poor-man's version of the former beauty. Her face, caked with makeup, couldn't hide the circles under her eyes. And her perfume, thick enough to choke out the stuffy air in the elevator, couldn't mask the smell of cigarettes on her breath. She looked like she hadn't slept in two days.

John thought of last night's sighting outside the gentlemen's club. Jenny hadn't been playing it cool with Apollo. She hadn't been acting. She was—

He leapt into the elevator and wrapped his arms around her, unwilling to go there in his head. "You're alive!"

"Uh-huh," she said and pulled away.

She was nervous, evasive, like an addict too skittish to make eye contact during and interrogation.

He grasped her shoulder with one hand. "Are you all right?"

"Sure," she said, still not looking him in the eye.

She felt cold and unresponsive to the touch, and the sight of her laughing it up with Apollo last night in the parking lot flashed through his head.

"What did they do to you?"

"Nothing," she said and hit the *open* button before the doors could close. She twisted free of his grasp and started for the dark corridor.

John hurried after her and grabbed her by the same arm. "Wait! Jenny, we've got to get you out of here!"

"Let go of me," she said and jerked her arm free. "I don't belong to you."

John chased after her once again and this time stood between her and the final stretch of hallway that led to Bloodgood Booking.

"Look, I saw you last night with Apollo. I saw you ... *laughing.*" He tried to clear his head. "I don't know what's happened to you or what you're doing down here, but it's obvious you're not thinking straight. We need to get you out of here—now!"

"Chump," Jenny whispered to her feet.

"What?"

John felt the familiar clicking sensation in his ears again, only this time more violently. The dark corridor suddenly felt like it was closing in on him, and he fought the urge to panic.

"I called you a fucking chump," she said and finally returned his gaze.

Her eyes were empty black pools, and her face was contorted beyond recognition.

"Jenny?"

"Officer O'Meara?" she said mockingly and hit him square in the jaw.

The blow felt like it had been delivered on the business end of a sledgehammer, and John dropped to the floor, seeing stars. He reached for his jaw and felt nothing but throbbing pain.

He finally struggled to his feet. "That's *detective*."

"Whatever," she said and stared at him menacingly.

Keep moving, he thought. *Keep talking*. "Did I mention you look like shit?"

"Bite me," she said and swung with all her might at his face.

He ducked the blow and used her own momentum to send her reeling against the far wall.

"If you're what I think you are, somebody already has."

"Yeah, well, look at me now," she said and motioned for him to bring it on. "I can sure as hell kick your out-of-shape ass."

"I thought you said I looked good for my age," John said, ducking the back of her hand.

"That was then," Jenny said. "This is now."

Preoccupied with her flailing fists, John didn't see her Day-Glo jogging shoe until it was planted firmly in his groin.

He groaned and fell to the floor, instinctively reaching for his aching privates.

She kicked him again, this time putting him on his back.

All he could do was roll with the impact and then groan and writhe under the steady rain of blows that followed.

"You know what you are, O'Meara?" she asked, pausing long enough to gloat over him. "You're a frickin' pervert. I mean, my God! What kind of cop lays someone in the throes of post-traumatic stress disorder? You barely had me out of that freakin' basement before you put your dick in me. You're old enough to be my dad for Christ's sake."

As much pain as he was in, John hurt worse knowing that sweet Jenny had been reduced to a monster. He hated Apollo with everything he had.

"Your sister's with Vladimir by the way," Jenny hissed as she kicked him in the ribs. "He says she's his favorite playmate."

John rolled onto his side and coiled into a protective ball. "You're lying," he choked out.

"Am I?" she said. "I hear she rides him like a fucking horse."

She was trying to provoke him or humiliate him before she put him away, but he had no plans to let her do either. She rolled him over and squatted on his stomach, temporarily knocking the wind out of him.

"You know what I think?" she said, grinding her pelvis into his gut. "I think you're a sorry old man so hard up you probably wanna ride *me* one last time—just for posterity."

"Not quite, sweetheart," John said with a grimace. "I wanna save you."

She smiled a wicked smile. "You're pathetic."

But her grin quickly went south when he jammed the oversized pencil Bettencourt had given him into her beautiful chest. She let out a moan and gasped for air, her eyes bulging in disbelief. "What the fuck? What are you trying to do to me?"

John pried the fancy pencil free and, fighting the gag reflex, thrust it into her chest again, this time entering below the sternum and angling upward, with a direct line to her once generous and open heart.

"Put you out of your misery," he answered through gritted teeth.

But the maneuver proved no easy task and was accomplished instead in agonizing stages, Jenny desperately grasping at his wrist with both of her hands and John looking away as he slowly drove the pencil home. He cried out with her when it finally broke off in her heart.

CHAPTER 14

JOHN STOPPED SHORT of his car, fell to his hands and knees, and retched. The relief was total. For a moment, he didn't know where he was or what he had done.

But the moment passed.

He wiped his mouth and struggled to his feet, his head still swarming with stars. The subterranean coolness of the parking garage, comforting a few minutes earlier, now felt alien.

He looked down at his shirt and saw that he was bathed in sweat, not to mention his girlfriend's blood.

That wasn't Jenny, he tried to tell himself.

But the facts didn't erase the crushing, almost paralyzing ache he felt inside. He wanted desperately to rewrite history, to undo that fateful night in the Lower Ninth Ward, where he had saved Jenny's life, only to unnecessarily and irresponsibly put her in harm's way just a few days later. But nothing could change the facts. Because of him, she had been reduced to a monster. Because of him, she had died twice—the last time in excruciating pain. And Payton. He refused to believe what Jenny had said about her. He would find her. He just had to get to Vladimir and wrench that scrawny neck of his to get at the truth.

He ducked his head into the VW and sat in silence. He

put the keys in the ignition and was about to turn the engine over when a champagne-colored limousine appeared in his rearview mirror, heading straight for him and the elevator bay. He ducked down as best he could and then waited, hoping to catch a glimpse of whomever it was that was lurking behind the tinted windows.

The limo pulled to a stop outside the elevator less than fifty feet away, and the driver emerged. Well groomed and carrying himself confidently, he wore a navy blue suit and could have easily passed for a successful businessman or politician.

Who's the VIP?

The answer came shortly as the driver opened the rear passenger's side door and out came ... the mayor. John recognized his face from the photo in the morning's paper. The fine features, the full head of hair, the charismatic smile—he looked just as dashing in real time as he did on the front page of the newspaper.

As his chauffeur leaned against the hood of the limo, the mayor walked the short distance to the elevators, pushed a button, and waited.

And then John's cell phone chirped.

He nearly jumped out of his seat, hurriedly pressing the talk button and then stealing a furtive glance at the mayor and his driver. Neither seemed alerted to his presence, the chauffeur chewing on one of his fingernails and the mayor bouncing on the balls of his feet as he waited for an elevator.

"O'Meara," John whispered into his phone.

"Detective, this is Angela Ramirez."

"Hey," he said curtly.

"Did I catch you at a bad time?"

"Uh-huh."

"Why are you whispering?"

"In the middle of something."

"Do you want me to call you back in a few minutes?"

"No," he said. "I'll call you."

153

John hung up just as the mayor was disappearing inside the elevator. He wondered how long the mayor would be gone, and he could tell by the bored look on the chauffeur's face that he was pondering the same thing. But as the elevator doors closed, John found himself suddenly gripped by panic.

Jenny!

The fear disappeared as quickly as it came. He had instinctively worried that Mayor Ward would stumble upon Jenny's body as soon as he entered the dark corridor to Bloodgood Booking, assuming that was where he was indeed heading, but there was nothing left of Jenny for the mayor to discover. She had exploded into dust the moment Bettencourt's oversized pencil had struck her heart. Her death had been as surreal as her metamorphosis.

The mayor emerged from the elevator a few minutes later, said something to his chauffeur, and then disappeared inside the limo.

As soon as the limo was gone, John redialed Angela.

"Hey," he said as soon as she picked up. "Any idea why the mayor would be hanging out in the warehouse district and paying a visit to Bloodgood Booking?"

"Good question," Angela said. "Why don't you ask him yourself tonight?"

"What do you mean?"

Angela laughed. "Let me back up a bit. How would you like to be my date at a party tonight?"

He looked down at Jenny's blood, which was still spattered on his T-shirt and blue jeans. "I'm not really in the partying mood."

"You will be when I tell you who's hosting."

"Who?" he asked impatiently.

"None other than Mr. Vladimir Frumos himself. He's throwing a little cocktail party at his penthouse downtown. The guest list is a mile long and includes the mayor."

John sat up stiffly in his seat. "You think he'll show?"

"I doubt it, but we won't know for sure until tonight," Angela answered. "I'll pick you up at eight. And detective?"

"Yeah?"

"Wear a tie."

~~~

If he hadn't just killed his girlfriend, John might have had a different reaction to Angela as she appeared in his motel room doorway dressed in an elegant sequin dress, complete with spaghetti straps and high heels, but all he felt was remorse.

"Wow," Angela said. "You look like someone just died."

He ignored the accuracy of her comment and followed her outside.

"Anything I can do?" she asked as they lingered in front of her car.

"No," he said and then corrected himself. "Just keep on looking beautiful. You're a sight for sore eyes."

"Thank you. I was starting to wonder if I'd lost my touch." She glanced at his rumpled jacket and open-collared shirt. "You'll never get through the lobby looking like that. Here," she said, reaching into her purse and pulling out a man's tie. "I figured you wouldn't have one. Compliments of the house."

John took it. "Thanks," he said. "I don't think I even own a tie."

They drove in silence for a few minutes before Angela said, "I'm curious what you've dug up since you got here. Any leads worth following yet?"

"No, but I've learned Pudge was right about one thing."

"What might that be?"

"Vampires die hard."

"What? You killed one of them?" Angela's eyes widened. "Who? Was it one of Vladimir's thugs?"

"Not exactly." John was tempted to fill Angela in on everything, including the part about Jenny exploding into dust, but it would take too much energy—and hurt too much. Besides, clamming up was more his style. "I'll tell you later."

They arrived at the entrance to Vladimir's luxury downtown condominium and were escorted to a long row of elevators by a carrot-topped bellhop.

"This place is amazing," Angela said, gaping at the posh lobby.

One of the elevators opened, and an attendant inside held the door for them as they entered.

John took in the opulence with a healthy dose of skepticism. "Since when does a house magician earn enough to live like this?"

"Good question," Angela said as the doors closed. "Regular gigs at Vegas pay well, especially when you're at the top of the marquee, but this kind of living is for millionaires fifty times over. Vladimir must have another gig on the side."

"Or friends in high places."

The elevator slowed to a stop at the thirteenth floor, the top floor, and the doors opened to reveal a penthouse as luxurious as anything John had ever seen. The coved ceilings, at least twenty feet high, were embossed in gold detail, and the stucco walls paid subtle backdrop to highbrow and high-priced paintings and sculptures, all of the art prominently displayed on pedestals or under lights. The foyer was softly lit, its black and gray tiles and dark walls looking like a cross between Gothic and ultramodern chic.

"Enjoy the party," the attendant said as the elevator closed.

John nodded without looking back.

There were a dozen or so guests lingering in the huge foyer, which felt more like a museum than a home, but the noise coming from one of the wide, arched doorways to their right showed where most of the partygoers had congregated.

"You could get lost in here," Angela said.

Indeed, the entryway reminded John of an M.C. Escher painting, minus the crisscrossing staircases. "Ten, eleven, twelve … I count fourteen doors and at least as many mirrors."

Angela closed her hand around John's and whispered into his ear, "What's a vampire need with so many mirrors?"

The warmth of contact was irresistible, and he instantly thought of Jenny. The pit in his stomach grew deeper.

They finally walked the length of the long, confusing foyer and arrived in a grand banquet room, complete with attendants serving hors d'oeuvres and cocktails on trays. Vladimir, dressed in a black tuxedo with long coattails, was at center court, entertaining a gaggle of attractive ladies, but he stopped as soon as he spotted Angela and the detective.

"Ah," he said and made his way through the crowd, "if it isn't Ms. Angela Ramirez, the intrepid reporter hot on the mayor's tail." He winked at John and then continued to address Angela. "The mayor has yet to grace us with his presence, although I am sure you noticed his name on the guest list I had faxed to your desk earlier today."

"I did," she said. "You probably hoped with the last-minute invite that I wouldn't be able to come."

Vladimir feigned surprise at the comment. "Absolutely not, *mademoiselle*." He frowned at John. "Although I dare say you might have found a more suitable companion."

John's bullshit meter was running full throttle in the red. "Give it a rest, Vlad," he said between clinched teeth. "You know why I'm here."

Vladimir appeared bored by the intrusion. "Hoping to find out more about your sister, I presume." He smiled toothily and then looked past John toward the entrance at the latest arrival. "Chief Lowman, you made it. Won't you join us?"

John turned to see Lowman, decked out in an ill-fitting suit and tie, and a smartly dressed woman, his wife perhaps, approaching. "Shit," he said under his breath and glanced at Angela, whose olive-toned face was burning crimson.

"Good evening, Mr. Frumos," the portly chief said. "Nice to meet you … again."

"Better than in an interrogation room, no?" Vladimir winked at the chief. "I am sure you know Ms. Ramirez."

The chief nodded to Angela and smiled curtly.

"… and Detective O'Meara."

Chief Lowman adjusted his belt, which was working overtime to hold in his gut, and glowered at John. "Detective," he said and glanced around the room. He returned his gaze to John. "Does your captain know you're in Las Vegas?"

"Nope," John lied. "He doesn't tell us how to spend our weekends."

"Good policy," the chief said. "But in your case, he'd be wise to use a shorter leash."

"Gentlemen," Vladimir said, interrupting the hostilities. "And ladies." He paused to offer an engaging smile to Angela and the woman on Chief Lowman's arm. "Please excuse me." He motioned to one of his attendants across the room. "I believe that good man over there is holding a martini that belongs to me."

And with that, the magician made an elegant exit, leaving John and the chief to trade venomous stares.

"Chief Lowman," Angela said. "I was wondering if you'd have time for a quick interview. Off the record, of course."

The bluster on the chief's face suddenly morphed into discomfort. "Uh, not tonight, Ms. Ramirez. I'm here strictly as a citizen. But maybe another time." He guided his date to the other side of the room, throwing one last menacing look John's way.

As soon as Chief Lowman was out of earshot, John turned to Angela, who was smiling mischievously. "You're good."

She shrugged her shoulders nonchalantly. "It works every time."

John glanced around the room, which was overflowing

with socialites. "Somehow I doubt the mayor will be making an appearance tonight."

"I think you're right," Angela said with a smile. "The last thing he wants after being indicted is to be spotted with this crowd."

Someone cleared his throat behind them, and John turned to see Alistair Bishop, who had a martini in one hand and an unlit cigarette in the other, frowning at them.

"And what's wrong with tonight's attendees?" Alistair asked, raising an eyebrow at Angela. He was wearing pajamas again, this time chartreuse.

The guy looks like a leprechaun, John thought.

Angela inhaled through her teeth and glanced askew at the floor. "Nothing, Mr. Bishop. I just have a hunch that, well, with all the mayor's ... *problems*, he needs to keep a low profile right now."

"And whose fault is that, young lady?"

Angela folded her arms defensively. "If you're insinuating that I've been on a witch hunt, you're gravely mistaken. I'm a newspaper reporter just doing my job. If the mayor was running a clean ship, he wouldn't be under investigation by the state's attorney general."

"Fair enough," Alistair said, abandoning his inquisitorial tone. He didn't seem the type to hold a grudge, much less make a scene at a party. "But I wish you knew the mayor like I do. He's a good person beneath it all, and he deserves our compassion. You can't imagine the pressures he faces every day. Others would have broken by now."

Angela's expression softened. "I'm sure you're right, Mr. Bishop," she said. "Perhaps you would be willing to sit down with me sometime and give me your take."

"Perhaps," Alistair said, his eyes narrowing. He glanced at John. "I've seen this gentleman somewhere before."

John nodded. "At Vladimir's show last night. We sat at the same table."

"Right you are!" Alistair enthused. "And what a fabulous show it was! Vladimir was spot on."

"Out of this world," John said.

"Well," Alistair said, "I think I'll wander off now before I say something incriminating in front of our reporter friend here."

John smirked at Angela, and the two stood silently as the old man tottered off in his pajamas.

"He's—"

"Eccentric," Angela said, finishing John's thought. "But very endearing. I hope he'll talk to me for real someday."

"I wouldn't count on it. Loyalty usually beats honesty when the two go head to head."

"You're probably right. So," Angela said with her hands on her hips and a devilish smile on her face, "what do you say we split up and do a little mingling? I'll give you a running commentary on all the VIPs later."

"You sure you feel safe alone with these vultures?"

Angela batted her eyes playfully. "Why, detective, are you saying I can't hold my own with a bunch of compulsive gamblers and smarmy politicians?"

"Watch your back," John said and left the banquet hall by a side door that led back to the foyer.

He had hoped to find more comfortable terrain, but he was quickly reminded of the foyer's disorienting layout. It looked nothing like the giant room he'd first seen upon exiting the elevator.

"Wild, isn't it?"

He turned to see who was speaking, and there *she* was, standing beside one of Vladimir's prized paintings, a martini in her hand and a pout on her lips. She wore a shimmering black minidress whose hemline looked short enough to lay waste to the tiniest of skirts and whose paper-thin material could have passed for the flimsiest of slips.

"Sadie."

"That's me," she cooed. "How you doin', cowboy?"

"I've had better days."

She glanced away, revealing the whites of her eyes. "I'm sorry to hear that."

Every move, every gesture, every breath she took played to the fire he felt burning inside him, and yet he sensed in her a deep sadness, something at once inevitable and tragic. She was a car crash in the making.

"Do you still hate dancing, detective?"

He nodded. "Always will. But the *dancer* is something else."

She drew closer, close enough for him to smell the alcohol on her breath and see the moisture glistening on her lips. "So you think there's a chance for us."

"Maybe," he said, too afraid to believe it.

"What would the world have to look like?"

"As beautiful as you."

"You think I'm beautiful?"

"Like the wide open road."

"But you think I'm … inscrutable."

He felt the waves of his dream pouring over him. "I wonder—"

"You wonder what?"

"I can't help wondering if you're real."

She dropped her gaze, as if she was absorbing some devastating piece of news, and then looked back up at him, tears welling in her hazel eyes. As she gazed intently at him, a look of resolve spread across her delicate face. She set her martini on a stone pedestal, nearly tipping it over in her haste, and then pulled him away from the painting on display and into a dark corner. "Let me show you."

She brought her lips to his, and the detective could feel himself slipping away. To where, he didn't care. He closed his eyes as she fumbled with his belt, trying to pry him loose. He could see the blood-red sea from his dreams coming straight for him.

This isn't real.

She slipped his hands beneath her hemline, and he skidded deeper into the dripping abyss.

Nothing is.

They were beneath the giant sycamore now, the dappled noon sun spilling through its canopy in slender slivers of light, and he had her pressed against the trunk, her legs wrapped around him as she gently rocked. Memories from his childhood—a lazy afternoon in the hammock, a tiny plane in the summer sky, croquet balls long since rolled to a stop on the green lawn around him—unwound one at a time, each one breaking free on the breeze. He saw his tenth birthday party, his mother pulling a red velvet cake from the oven. He saw a bundle of newspapers in front of his driveway, each one rolled tightly in a faded red rubber band and ready for delivery. He saw the neighborhood bully, his sister shaking a clenched fist at him.

Payton.

She's safe.

How do you know?

I know.

He felt himself explode into a thousand tiny fragments, bliss caving in on itself, until nothing was left, and when he opened his eyes, there was Sadie, pinned between him and the stucco wall behind her, quietly moaning in the afterglow.

He eased her back down until her high heels were touching the black tiles and then zipped up his slacks self-consciously. He could hear Angela laughing in the room next door as she talked up one of the guests.

"What the hell was that?" he whispered.

Sadie ignored the question, her soft lips lingering on his neck. "Do me a favor, detective," she whispered as she brought her mouth to his ear. "Remember me like this, okay?"

"What do you mean?"

"Just remember," she said and pulled away from their

embrace. She turned to walk away and then paused briefly beneath a pale blue recessed light, her face half-cast in darkness. "Remember how beautiful the world looked."

"I don't understand," he said, but he was talking to the back of her blue-black bob as she disappeared into a small crowd of partygoers who had just wandered into the foyer.

"There you are!" Angela said. "I've been looking for you for the past hour."

He turned to see Angela staring at him from an open door. She pointed peevishly to the slender silver watch on her left wrist.

"Hour?" he asked in disbelief.

"And then some. I know I said I'd give you the rundown on a few VIPs, but it's getting late." She paused and threw him a curious look. "You okay?"

"Sure," he said, suddenly conscious of the sweat pooled on his forehead.

She took him by the arm. "Well, detective, I'm tired. I can only play the social game for so long. What do you say we blow this joint?"

He felt the weight of the world suddenly lift from his shoulders. "Let's."

After a short elevator ride, the two were back downstairs and then on the street once again. Angela looked deep in thought as they waited for the valet to arrive with her car.

"So," John said, his mind starting to clear, "why the quick exit? I figured we'd be the last to leave."

"Me too," Angela said, "but I'm dying to figure something out."

"What's that?"

"Who Randi Ward is."

"What?"

"A couple minutes before I found you in the foyer, I was walking around by myself, just sort of casually looking at some of the artwork. I was barely paying attention, because

I was mostly just trying to eavesdrop." She flashed a guilty smile. "Anyway, I was in front of a painting—just a landscape, and pretty dull by Vladimir's standards—when I noticed the artist's name at the bottom left-hand corner: Randi A. Ward. Randi with an *I*, mind you. I thought, *Gee, that's interesting. Change I to a Y, and you've got our mayor.*"

"Could be a coincidence."

"Detective, after everything you've seen, do you really believe in coincidences anymore?"

~~~

As soon as he was back in his hotel room, John called Billy Thune's cell number.

"This is Billy," his fellow cop answered groggily after the third ring.

"Billy, this is John."

"O'Meara?" Billy lowered his voice to just shy of a whisper. "Do you know what time it is? You'd better pray you didn't wake up little Josie, or Staci will be on the warpath."

"Sorry, buddy, I forgot about the time difference, but I need you to do some legwork for me tomorrow morning as soon as you get in."

"Like I don't have a shitload to do already. Captain's got us running our asses off since your little adventure."

"It'll just take a few minutes on the computer. I don't have a laptop with me and can't get into the network."

Silence.

Finally, Billy spoke. "Shit. All right. Give it to me."

"I need you to dig up everything you can on Randall A. Ward, mayor of Las Vegas. Birth certificate, places of residence, school history, marriage certificate or certificates—that kind of thing. Then I need you to hunt down a similar name: Randi A. Ward. Randi with an *I*."

"You got it, asshole. Anything else?"

"Sure. I'll have fries with that. And a shake."

Chapter 15

"YOU WORM!" JENNY was staring up at him from a black hole in the ground, six feet beneath the close-clipped grass, both feet planted squarely in her grave. "You did me wrong!"

"I—"

She leapt from the grave and tore at him with her fists. "You couldn't even *kill* me right," she seethed. "Now look at me!"

His former lover had tree roots for hair and a broken-tooth grimace, and she was shaking from head to toe in the moonlight like a junkie begging for one last fix.

He was about to respond when he heard someone behind him speak.

"You did the only thing you could. Mom and dad would be proud."

John turned to see Payton, her body, too, a decomposing mess. "Payton?"

"But what about me? Did you ever stop to think that while you were playing house with that poor innocent girl, I was being buried alive? Yeah, brother, I was alive once. Had big dreams, too, remember? And look at me now."

"Don't look at her."

He whirled to see Sadie wearing next to nothing and walking toward him in the grass.

"Look at me."

She was exquisite, from her delicate face to her slender bare feet; however, her cheeks were streaked with blood, which had dried to a shade as black as the night sky, and her right hand was holding something ... wrong.

John squinted at the object as she walked toward him. What was it? She had it by its hair, clumped and dripping blood.

You know him.

He grimaced at the sight of Pudge's decapitated head.

You killed him.

He tried to close his eyes.

You owe him.

John jerked himself awake and looked at the digital alarm clock on his nightstand, which said 2:41 AM. He threw off the sheets and shuffled to the bathroom for a drink of water. Another long night of dreaming lay ahead of him.

~~~

Sunday morning dawned brightly outside John's motel window, with clear skies as far as the eye could see. He took a quick shower and then stopped in the lobby for a cup of straight black coffee.

He was in the parking lot a couple minutes later and walking to his car when his cell phone rang. He checked the caller ID and recognized Angela's number.

"You're out of the gates quickly today," he said. "I'm impressed."

"I'm a morning person. What's your excuse?"

"I was just about to head to the casino for some more snooping."

"Hold that thought," Angela said. "I've got a bombshell I'd like to drop on you."

"Anything to do with your mayor?"

"It's funny," Angela said. "I've been digging up stuff on him for over a year, but when you're looking in the wrong places, nothing comes easy. On the other hand, if I would have just changed the parameters of my investigation a bit, maybe everything would have come into view a lot sooner, crystal clear and right in front of my nose the whole time."

John smiled. "You cracked the case."

"Nope," she said. "I got lucky. An anonymous … *tip*, I guess you'd call it. You'll have to see it to believe it."

An incoming call beeped in John's ear. "Damn it. Angela, can you hold a second? I've got someone on the other line."

"Sure, but make it quick."

"No sweat." John clicked over to the other line. "O'Meara."

"O'Meara, this is Billy."

"What took you so long? I'm about to get scooped by a reporter."

"Gee, sorry, bud. Next time, I'll just blow you off when you call me at home at midnight asking for favors. The only reason I'm working this weekend is to cover for your sorry ass."

John exhaled slowly. "Sorry. What'd you find out?"

"Well, for starters, your mayor ain't no man."

"What?"

"I mean, he's a she. Got a sex change when she was in her late teens right after dropping out of art school."

"Art school?"

"Right. The lady must have fancied herself a painter until she found Jesus. Then she did the surgery, and it was off to goddamned Oral Roberts University. After that, the dude got into local politics. City council—that kind of shit. Ask any reporter in town there about his past, and I guarantee they won't be able to locate him before Oral Roberts."

John thought of Angela on the other line and the bombshell awaiting him. *I bet I know one who can.*

"He probably has some bullshit bio up on his Web site," Billy continued, "about his happy childhood in small town

America, and I bet you those joker reporters all quote it verbatim. Shit, the guy's probably paid actors to pretend they're old chums of his."

"You've got to be pretty slick to keep a lie alive that long," John said. "Anything else?"

"That about covers it. I can fax you all the documents if you need."

"Do it. Send 'em to my hotel room. In the meantime, I've got someone on the other line. Thanks, Billy. You're the man."

"No shit."

John hung up with Billy and clicked over. "You still there, Angela?"

"I am," she said testily. "I was about to hang up."

"Sorry. Quick question. You said the first time we met that Mayor Ward and Alistair Bishop are old college chums. What college?"

Angela was silent for a moment. "Oral Roberts University, if I remember correctly."

"Really, Ms. Ramirez," John chided, "can you imagine Alistair Bishop at a fundamentalist Christian college?"

"No, I guess I can't. What are you getting at?"

"You're not the only one with big news."

Angela laughed. "It's about time, detective. I was beginning to wonder if you were just here for the dancing girls. What do you say we meet at my office in about fifteen minutes and compare notes? Don't be late."

John clicked off the phone and keyed the ignition. He wasn't sure where all this was leading, but it felt good to be finally getting somewhere. He tried to take solace in the old adage of the hare not always winning the race. If this was a marathon, he was prepared to play the role of the slow-moving tortoise and outlast everybody, but in his gut, he knew time wasn't on his side. Even if Payton was still okay, *he* wasn't. Between his dreams and his real encounters with Sadie, he was having a hard time distinguishing between what was actually real and what was horror. Even Vegas was starting to look more and more like a surreal fantasy than the empty shell game it was. The new revelations about the mayor only deepened the mystery.

But he'd barely backed out of his parking space when he was swearing a blue streak. "Damn it!" he growled and jerked the gearshift back into first gear.

As soon as he had reparked the car, he stepped outside to assess the damage. Someone had slashed one of his rear tires.

He opened the hatchback to search for a spare tire and jack.

Looks like I'll be late.

~~~

Angela gathered her notes and took one last sip of coffee. She thought about Detective O'Meara. Could he be trusted fully? She wished she knew more about him: his work habits, his politics, his personality. It was clear he felt some loyalty to Pudge and wanted to solve the missing girls' case, but how far did his loyalty extend? His bottom line was clearly finding his sister. If he found her, would he stay on the case or be on the first flight back home?

As she rinsed her coffee cup in the kitchen sink, she felt the skin on her neck rise suddenly. The eerie chill was followed by a strange, claustrophobic sensation in her ears. She'd experienced the same feeling once before. But where? She watched helplessly as the porcelain cup slipped through her fingers and shattered in the sink. She wanted to turn off the water but hesitated instead, frozen in fear.

A voice came to her on a fog. "Turn it off, and close the blinds."

She did as she was told but still stared straight ahead, afraid to turn around.

"Now … come to me." The voice sounded closer now, as if it was emanating from somewhere in her apartment.

She found herself jerking around, marionette-like, but who was pulling the strings? Her body felt like it belonged to somebody else, and she could feel her sudden lack of independence squarely in her gut, which was alive with butterflies.

"Come closer." The disembodied voice was barely a whisper now.

She tried to speak but felt too weak to open her mouth.

But where?

Here.

She saw her bedroom, lights off and blinds drawn, in her mind's eye and felt herself being pulled toward it. Her legs were like stone but carried her just the same.

Once in the doorway, she saw someone standing at the foot of her bed, an oily shadow she'd seen once before.

Where?

Here.

As she struggled against the phantom, which was threatening to own not only her will but her thoughts, she had a flash of recognition.

I know you.

Silence.

No.

She tried to muster the strength to turn and run, but she felt like she did in every nightmare she'd ever had since childhood. Fear felt like quicksand, and evil was faceless but loomed frighteningly near, suffocating in its proximity.

I know you.

The stranger drew her to him and lifted her face slowly upward until their eyes met, her chin resting on his bony index finger.

You know only what I tell you.

She felt a sudden, white-hot sensation streak across her neck and looked down in disbelief as the blood streaming from her wound turned her white, silk blouse a deep shade of red. She could hear a strange lapping sound and looked up in time to see him sucking her blood from the long fingernail at the end of his index finger. His eyes were unapologetic, neither lustful nor remorseful, and for the first time she understood she was dying—so someone else could live.

~~~

With the lobby closed on Sundays, John was forced to find a back door into the *Las Vegas Sun* newsroom through the press room. As he closed the heavy steel door behind him, he cut off the overpowering waft from the printing presses, but he was disappointed to find only a skeleton crew in the newsroom—and no Angela.

"What do you mean she hasn't shown up yet?" he asked a dowdy reporter staring up at him from her cubicle. "She said she was coming straight here."

"Maybe she's stuck in traffic."

"On a Sunday? I'll call her from my cell."

John dialed Angela's home number and waited. When she didn't answer, he punched in her cell number. It, too, went straight to voice mail after a few rings.

"Come on, reporter. Where are you?"

He stared at the black grease on his free hand, still left over from changing his tire back at the motel, and suddenly felt a queasy tingling in his gut—the same reaction that always gave him pause when his sick sense kicked in. Maybe Angela was late for a good reason.

He dialed Billy Thune back at the shop.

"Fifth District, this is Billy."

John breathed a sigh of relief at the quick answer. "Billy," he said, "I need another favor."

"Shit. What am I? Your goddamned secretary? What now?"

"I need you to look up an address for me—and type fast."

~~~

Vladimir let the reporter's lifeless body fall to the bed. She had died with her mouth hanging open, something he often found distasteful. His belly was full, but so was his conscience. He was not, despite how his act was portrayed onstage, a monster.

"I wonder if they make tofu for vampires," he said and wiped the last of her blood from his mouth.

She had been healthy, overflowing with vitality, in fact, which as usual left him to sort through a grab bag of mixed feelings. On the one hand, her blood was the best thing he could put into his body. On the other, she could have lived another forty or fifty happy years, all things being equal. Who needed to carry around that kind of guilt?

But guilt inevitably led to anger, as it always did. Why should he feel bad for feeding himself? Was his life less important than those of his victims? And *victim* was a loaded word. Who was really the victim here? The person who had died a relatively painless—and certainly quick—death, or the person who had authored the same awful scenario a thousand times?

I am a showman, he insisted to himself. *Not an uncouth murderer.*

Indeed, he had been forced to play the role of Ms. Ramirez's executioner, because circumstances had necessitated it. Debating it would have been pointless. Her nosiness—just like Officer Feineman's—had left him with no choice but to protect himself and his career. End of story.

So what if he cherished the view from the top of the mountain so much that he was willing to kill to keep it? Like every other entertainer out there, he had long resigned himself to living with certain … concessions, all of them forced upon him, if it meant he could continue making a handsome living from his art. He wasn't the only one to have sold his soul to the devil. Artists and others in the entertainment industry did it all the time—and for much less.

"Now," he said aloud, "what have you been up to, Ms. Ramirez?"

He thumbed through the reporter's spiral notebook and quickly decided a wholesale shredding was in order. As he tore the pages free a handful at a time and fed them to the shredder, he let his mind drift.

"Blood banks," he said aloud but then dismissed the notion. "No, we vampires prefer draft, not bottled blood."

He thought of the burgeoning niche within the hospice industry, one created almost solely by vampires (and a helpful contingent of ethically challenged humans), and how easy it was to order up a patient about to expire. Aging and infirmed vampires often counted on such services, greedily awaiting their next meals on wheels. Of course, human nature being what it was, there were often those among them who drank more than their share. But they were curbed, or failing that, weeded out.

His thoughts returned full circle. Tofu for vampires? It was a ludicrous idea in the end. There existed a tiny and haplessly ostracized minority of vegan vampires, pathetic individuals subsisting in the shadows who lived stunted lives on the blood of animals, but no one approved their lifestyle. They had rejected their own destiny. He vowed never to forsake his.

~~~

"Anybody home?"

John found the door to Angela's apartment slightly ajar and eased himself inside. He quietly closed the door behind him while he was careful not to leave any fingerprints behind. The place was eerily shut up, with all the blinds closed and no lights left on.

Wherever she is, he thought as he stuffed a handkerchief into his back pocket, *she's not here.*

It never felt right to invade someone's space even while he was doing police work, and he was tempted to turn around and go out the way he'd come. But a faint humming sound caught his attention.

He stepped into the white-tiled kitchen, but the sound faded.

Another potential clue then gave him pause.

What's that?

A small white shard lay at his feet, and he knelt to inspect it. A plate or a cup or something? But where was the rest of it? He stood up and walked to the sink, where he found a coffee cup or what was left of it in pieces in the drain. Angela had either been in a big hurry or—

He hurried down the hallway and stopped at the bedroom doorway.

She was sprawled atop her made bed, her mouth hanging open, her face the color of a pale blue Wisteria bloom. She had been cut from ear to ear. A red-black rosette stretched across the front of her blouse, but there was no evidence of splatter and no blood trail.

Where did the blood go?

He knew the answer before he asked the question.

On her floor lay her laptop, now in pieces. And above it on her dresser sat a shredding machine, still humming, and a mountain of shredded documents, the ribbons of paper still streaming down the side of the dresser and tumbling to the carpet below. Whatever Angela might have discovered had died with her.

John silenced the shredder by kicking its cord from the outlet.

No, damn it! Nobody's untouchable. You left something, and I'm gonna nail you with it.

He knelt down and studied the clutter of shredded paper, careful not to touch anything. He then shifted his attention to Angela's dead body, forgetting for the moment that she had been a colleague, maybe even a friend. He turned and saw her reflection on the television sitting atop a small table opposite her bed. She looked like a ghost, blue-white and blurred.

You left something behind. What was it?

He was tempted to tear the room apart, but he remembered the broken cup in the sink and retraced the killer's steps to the kitchen. Her murderer had come here not only to kill Angela but to erase her work. But a reporter kept notes everywhere, not just in notebooks. He tore a tissue free from a Kleenex dispenser on the counter and used it to open each drawer. Everyone had a utility drawer in their kitchen with notes, business cards, whatever. What had her murderer missed? When that search came up empty, he checked the notepad by her phone and then the various notes and photos tacked to her refrigerator with magnets.

He turned away from the refrigerator and searched his memory. What had she said about the bombshell she was hoping to drop on the mayor?

You'll have to see it to believe it.

See it to believe it.

He hurried to the living room and carefully opened the armoire but found only an empty space where the television should have been. Then he felt a chill on his spine as Angela's ghostlike image flashed through his mind. The television in her bedroom!

What was it Angela had said about breaking a story wide open? All someone had to do was look in the right direction. Then everything would fall into place. Her killer had tried to bury the trail that would lead John to him. But he, too, had been looking in the wrong places. Maybe he wasn't human, but nobody was untouchable. Even vampires made mistakes.

John sat at the foot of Angela's bed and carefully turned on the TV. The video sticking out a quarter of the way from the VCR went in without a fuss, and he sat in eerie silence only inches from Angela's cold body as he waited for the white fuzz to morph into the evidence that would bury every bloodsucker in Vegas.

CHAPTER 16

THE GIRL COULDN'T take her eyes off Vladimir as he drained her. Was she still alive? In shock? She lay limply in his arms as the magician noisily gulped from her neck, one hand wrapped around her shoulder and the other slithering up her blouse.

"So this isn't the first time this has happened to you?" a woman asked somewhere off screen, her voice sounding familiar to John.

The camera pulled back until Vladimir and his victim on the couch were a blurry background image. In the foreground was none other than Randall Ward, mayor of Las Vegas, stark naked other than the rouge lipstick streaked across his face and bound with leather straps to a spindly wood chair. Beside him stood Sadie, topless and holding a whip.

"No," the mayor said as tears rolled down his cheeks. "My wife and I haven't made love in months. I ... can't ... perform."

"Why?" Sadie asked and sat in his lap with her back to the camera. She churned her hips ever so slowly. "Don't you like me?"

The mayor ignored the question. "What's happening to that poor young girl behind me?"

"Oh, she'll be okay," Sadie answered for Vladimir, who

was still busily bleeding the girl dry. "We're more concerned about you." Sadie stood up slowly, her back still to the camera, and paraded in front of the mayor. "I mean, most men, if they were real men, would do anything for a taste of this."

"You already know my story," the mayor said bitterly. "Why are you torturing me?"

Behind them, a blurry Vladimir let the dead girl slide from his lap to the floor and then got up from the couch to join Sadie beside the mayor.

"May I?" he asked, wiping his mouth.

"Be my guest," Sadie said and walked off camera.

"Because, Mr. Mayor," Vladimir answered, "we need insurance. Can you see that camera there?" He pointed toward the viewer.

The mayor nodded feebly.

"That, my dear mayor, is our insurance. We want you to share your secret with us. And we promise to keep it forever … so long as you promise to keep ours to your grave."

"I promise."

"There, there, Mr. Mayor. You have not shared your secret yet. Please. We're waiting."

The mayor shook his head slowly. "I have trouble performing because … I'm … not … a man."

"Go on."

"I was born a woman," the mayor said through tears.

"Why on earth did you change who you were?" Vladimir asked. "Certainly you made a fine woman."

"I lusted … in my heart … for women."

"So?" Vladimir asked with a shrug.

"As someone who was born again, I couldn't reconcile my love of women with my love of Jesus Christ. Homosexuality is a sin in God's eyes."

"So you had an operation? Why not just join a convent or take a vow of chastity?"

The mayor sighed. "I foolishly thought that if I were a man—"

"Your love for women would suddenly be beautiful in the eyes of the Lord?"

"Something like that."

Vladimir grabbed the mayor by his full head of hair and forced him to look at the camera. "And now?"

"Now I am the father of four adopted children and have been married to the same wonderful woman for twenty-six years, but the lust has not left me. I have had multiple affairs despite becoming increasingly … dysfunctional."

"Why not take Viagra?" the magician said in mock concern. "Virility can be yours again."

"It's not that simple. My hormones are off the charts. I'm all fucked up."

"Because you were meant to be a woman. Because God wanted you to be a woman."

The mayor nodded in shame.

"There," Vladimir said and let go of his hair. "That was not so terribly hard, was it?"

In the blurry background, Sadie reappeared briefly as she dragged the dead girl off camera.

CHAPTER 17

THE SUN WAS just going down as John pulled into the underground parking lot at Bloodgood Booking. He found a parking spot between two other cars with a view of the elevators and then cut the engine.

It was tempting to feel sorry for the mayor despite everything he'd done. True, he had allowed himself to be blackmailed, and innocent people had died in order to protect his political career, which was already threatening to implode, with or without the damaging revelations from the videotape being aired to the public. But it was clear that he wasn't a bad man, just a weak one. To his supporters, he was the Rock of Gibraltar, steady and true in the face of an increasingly secular and profane world, but behind closed doors, he was horribly human: passionate yet insecure, idealistic yet craven. He had tried to retool his identity, only to lose himself entirely.

John frowned like someone who'd just stepped in excrement. How had he gotten himself into such a mess? He had come to Vegas to find his sister only to lose a fellow cop, kill his girlfriend, and now discover the dead body of a crackerjack reporter. If the mayor was a fraud, what was he? He shuddered at the comparison. At least he wasn't a parasite like Vladimir. Or a temptress. The image of Sadie topless and

179

holding a whip was impossible to shake loose, but he was glad for it. It would make his job that much easier. Since their first encounter, she had kept him on his heels. Now he knew what he had to do.

The first chore would be to confront Eugene Bettencourt. The booking agent knew more, of that John was certain, and he'd be less evasive out here in the relative open than in his creepy little basement office.

The sound of squealing tires caught John's attention, and he glanced in his rearview mirror just in time to see the mayor's champagne-colored limousine rounding the corner behind him, parking lights on and windows dimmed.

"What the—"

John sunk below the head rest and waited for the stretch limo to go by. This time, he was far enough away from the elevators that he wasn't too concerned about being spotted, but his curiosity had definitely been piqued.

Jesus. The mayor might as well keep regular office hours here.

He chuckled quietly to himself but then frowned just as quickly when he caught sight of Sadie emerging from the elevator bay, escorted by Bettencourt himself. She was dressed conservatively, in a pair of faded blue jeans and a black chemise.

The mayor's limo arrived at the bay just as Bettencourt was waving good-bye to Sadie and trudging off to his car, coffee thermos and black cap in hand. The guy truly was old school. Even his wheels, a '70s Austin Healey, evoked a long-past era in the entertainment industry.

Sadie waved at the booking agent and then waited for the all-business chauffeur to open the rear door of the limousine.

John made an easy decision and shifted his attention from Bettencourt, his initial focus, to Sadie and the mayor.

Inside the limo, his profile clearly visible beneath the dome light, sat the mayor, looking awfully relaxed for a guy who'd been caught on videotape confessing his true identity while naked and tied to a chair.

Sadie ducked inside, and the chauffeur closed the door and waited beside the limo.

What are you up to now, girl?

The meeting lasted maybe sixty seconds, long enough for Bettencourt to drive off in his Austin Healey, before Sadie emerged from the limo with a serene smile on her face. The mayor, rubbing his neck and looking about as confident as a wet rag, nodded to the chauffeur and was whisked away as quickly as he'd come.

Sadie began walking the length of the parking lot, her beautiful hips churning, and John squinted at the far wall, surprised to see her black Mercedes.

How did I miss that? he wondered as she opened her purse to retrieve her keys.

Before he could answer the question, Apollo's ugly mug was staring at him through the other side of the passenger's window.

John reached for the door, forgetting the VW had automatic locks, but was too slow, and Apollo was able to force his way inside.

"You killed my partner," Apollo growled as he clamped his hands around John's throat. "I told you I wouldn't forget."

"Listen, Apollo," John said, struggling to pry himself free of the bruiser's iron grip, "I don't have time for this right now."

"You ain't got time to die?"

"No," John said and let go with one hand. "I don't have time to clean up this car. It's a rental."

Apollo's eyes, only inches from his, narrowed as his bushy eyebrows met. "What the fuck you talkin' about, cop?"

John finally pulled his gun free and placed the barrel under Apollo's freshly shaved chin. "Well, Einstein, if I pull the trigger, I'm going to make a hell of a mess."

The bouncer looked down at the gun pointed at his chin and loosened his grip.

"I want you to back out, tough guy, the same way you came in."

Apollo loosened his grip further. "This ain't over, asshole."

"Let's hope for both of our sakes it is," John said. He was about to wave Apollo out of his car when the underground parking lot suddenly lit up with another car's headlights. "Now what?"

"Fuck a duck," Apollo grunted. "More cops!"

John didn't dare take his eyes off the bouncer. "How many?"

"One unmarked patrol car. Probably your buddies."

"I don't have any friends in Vegas, remember?"

"That's right," Apollo said, his eyes widening at the realization. "I don't need to wax you. The cops'll do it for me."

"Doubt it," John said. "Cop-on-cop murders rarely go down well at the precinct."

"Who's gonna know it was a cop? I sure as hell ain't gonna squeal."

"Apollo," John began in an annoyed tone and then stopped himself. "Is that really your name?"

The bruiser, his face still only inches away from John's, looked confused. "What's it to you?"

"Just curious," John said as he pushed his gun a little deeper into his chin.

"Ouch," Apollo said. "You're getting awfully touchy with that thing."

"Sorry," John said, "just wanted to make sure you remembered it was there."

John heard the patrol car slow to a stop beside his car. With his back to the driver's side window, he was able to steal a peek of the unmarked car, which was now even with the back window.

"Shit," he said as soon as he recognized Detective Pettit behind the wheel and the car's lone occupant. "Not him. Anybody but him."

"Pal of yours?"

"The opposite," John said.

John stole another furtive glance and saw Pettit working the radio. "Looks like we're going to have more company shortly."

The door to Pettit's car opened, and he stepped out cautiously.

Just as the detective was placing his hand on his holster, Apollo made a grab for John's gun inside the car. What followed was a desperate struggle for the gun, Apollo manhandling the barrel and John maintaining his grip on the handle. The bruiser was at least twice as strong as John but didn't seem to understand basic physics or the principles behind leverage. He did, though, have an intimate knowledge of low blows and was using his knee, his elbows, and his forehead with violent effectiveness. John was just trying to hold onto his gun. If he could weather the storm of blows and still keep his presence of mind—

The gun went off, and Apollo's body was suddenly nothing but dead weight. The blast deafened him for a moment.

John opened the door behind him and squirmed free, landing with his hands first and then his knees on the pavement. He looked up to see the barrel of Detective Pettit's gun.

"O'Meara," Pettit said with a nod. "You working tonight, or just enjoying another weekend in Vegas?" The gangly cop with a boxer's chin didn't wait for an answer. "Who's your friend?"

As John slowly rose to his feet, Pettit tossed him a rag. "Here," he said. "Clean up. You look like shit." John dabbed self-consciously at the blood splatters on his face.

"Excuse me, gentlemen." Both men turned to see Sadie standing in the middle of the parking lot, keys in hand, a perfect pout on her lips.

"I hate to interrupt," she cooed, "but my car won't start. I was hoping Detective O'Meara could give me a ride back to my place."

"My car's a bit of a … mess at the moment," John said. "Maybe Detective Pettit can assist you."

The look on Detective Pettit's face told John that he didn't appreciate the suggestion and that he knew well who Sadie was. He opened his mouth to protest, but Sadie cut him off.

"That's all right, detective," Sadie said to John. "I'm not squeamish. I can ride in the back."

"Suit yourself," John said and turned to get into his car.

"Hold on a minute," Pettit said. "You can't just—"

"Sure he can," Sadie said. "You saw what I saw. The detective was protecting himself against one of my overprotective bodyguards."

"But—"

Sadie rolled her eyes. "Have Chief Lowman call the mayor's office. I'm sure between the two of them they can sort this mess out."

John ducked inside and pushed Apollo's body against the opposite door, making sure that he was well below the window.

Sadie let herself in behind John and then waved to Detective Pettit. "Don't worry, detective. You're not in trouble."

John threw Pettit an ornery grin and then drove forward through the empty parking space in front of him and toward the garage's exit. He'd only traveled a block when two patrol cars flew by going in the opposite direction.

"Sorry about Apollo," Sadie said. "He wasn't so bright, but he was loyal to the end."

"Why didn't you try to stop him? He could still be young and dumb, and I wouldn't have to figure out what to do with his body." John shook his head as he spied blood on the ceiling, the dash, the steering column. "Know anyone who details cars?"

Sadie laughed. "I'm sure you'll find a way out of your current predicament, detective. You always do."

John glanced in his rearview mirror and saw Sadie smiling at him, her beautiful hazel eyes all lit up. He felt the familiar dreamy sensation, the deep longing, the spell she was so good at casting, and he closed his eyes. Tonight would be different.

"So," he said, "where's your whip?"

Sadie's eyes widened, and her cheeks flushed red. For once, she was speechless, her mouth hanging open in disbelief.

Finally, she spoke. "I thought he destroyed everything."

"You would have liked that," John said. "But ol' Vlad missed the videotape sitting, oh, about eight feet away from Angela after he killed her."

"No," Sadie said. "You don't get it. I—"

"Save it," John said. "I know who you are." He threw her a sarcastic frown. "I can see your soul."

"What are you going to do?" she asked.

"I'm going to drop you off at your place just like you asked," he said. "Then I'm going to pay one last visit to Vladimir ... and settle it."

"No!" Sadie said. "He'll tear you to pieces!"

"I doubt it," John said. "I kill people like him all the time. It's what I do."

"He doesn't have your sister," Sadie blurted out.

John screeched to a stop on the side of the road, killed the ignition, and turned to face Sadie. "What do you know about my sister?" he snarled.

Sadie shrunk from him. "Nothing. Nobody knows a thing about your sister! She and Vladimir never met."

John weighed the tone of her voice, the pleading look in her eyes and almost believed her for a second.

"Bullshit," he hissed. "Vladimir knows something, and

I'm going to pry it out of him before I shove something pointy through his heart. And listen to this, sister. If you try to get between us, if you try to save your lover-boy or your master or whatever the hell he is, you're going down with him." He looked away and spoke just loud enough for her to hear him. "I've already had to kill one vampire. I can do it again."

~~~

He could hear them laughing. Clinking their glasses and toasting the future. Cutting into their veal and savoring the first bite. Delighting in tiny turns of phrases, the kind of chitchat bullshit that made well-to-do snobs all sticky in their pants. One man's aphrodisiac was another man's poison, and Vladimir and his dining companions were enough to send John scurrying for a bedpan.

John had found it simple to enter the penthouse. All he had done was slip a few bucks to the bellhop and the elevator attendant, and he was in. He kicked open the swinging door that led from the service entrance into the long dining hall and didn't stop until he'd reached the head of the table, where the father of their feast was regaling his fawning fans and companions.

The others choked on their wine and sunk into their chairs, but the magician sat still without flinching, a wine glass still in his hand and John's gun at his temple.

"Why, detective," Vladimir said, affecting the over-dignified persona that served him so well onstage and off, "I do not remember seeing your name on tonight's guest list."

"No?" John asked and glanced around the long table at the other guests, all of them recoiling from him in horror. "I don't see anyone from the editorial board at the *Las Vegas Sun*, either. I guess they're too busy burying their best reporter."

Vladimir looked away nervously before he quickly recovered his composure. "I am afraid I do not know what you are talking about, detective."

"Let me refresh your memory then, Vlad. When you were

putting Angela's notebooks through the shredder this morning, did you notice the TV across the room? Probably not. If you had, you wouldn't have left your little snuff film—or was that a porn flick?—sitting in the VCR."

The magician glanced down at his plate, red-faced and clearly on the verge of exploding. He slowly lifted his gaze to the others. "My friends, I apologize for the intrusion. My friend here has been under a great deal of pressure since his sister disappeared. I think it's best that we bring tonight's gathering to an end so that I might tend to him." He glanced sympathetically at John and then back to the others, a toothy smile replacing the frown on his face. "Do not fret. There is always tomorrow. I've enough red wine to keep us stocked until the Rapture."

Vladimir's guests laughed nervously, dropped their napkins in their plates, and made a hasty exit.

As soon as the last dinner guest had left, Vladimir glared up at John, who was still pointing his gun at his head.

The magician took his time draining the last of his red wine and then scowled. "You must know by now how useless such a weapon is against me."

"Maybe it can't kill you," John said as he massaged the trigger, "but I'm sure it hurts something special."

"Perhaps," Vladimir said, "but you cannot shoot what you cannot see."

John felt the room closing in around him and pulled the trigger as fast as he could, but the magician was already gone. He stumbled over a chair as he bolted for the door to the foyer, his ears ringing.

"Damn it!" he said and picked himself back up.

He felt a fluttering in his head and suddenly felt the urge to vomit.

"Detective, did you really think you could kill me so easily?"

"Killing's never easy," he said and hurried toward the foyer.

"But in your case, I'm pretty sure I can pull the trigger with a clean conscience."

"First you must find me."

"Not a problem. All I have to do is follow the stink."

"Very funny, detective. But your sophomoric humor cannot rattle a man of my caliber."

"Man? I thought you were an animal."

This time, the joke earned no response.

John studied the labyrinthine foyer in dismay. There were enough doors and causeways to paralyze him, but he forged deeper into the enormous hallway. It didn't matter which way he went. Vladimir would find him.

The room, backlit with soft lights and showcasing a tangle of paintings and sculptures, each in its own nook, made for the perfect maze. But if he was the bait, he was also the lure. He would try to find the best place to trap the magician.

A strange ringing sound punctuated the silence, and then all was quiet once again.

What the hell was that?

John stood silently, trying to hone in on the sound's origin.

The ringing sound came again, and he suddenly realized its source.

Son of a bitch!

He reached for his cell phone and stole a quick glimpse of the caller ID. With his heart pounding in his ears and his gun practically ready to go off by itself, it was hard to clear his head long enough to recognize the number stretched across his caller ID readout. But how could he forget a number he knew by heart, one that was practically scratched into his DNA?

"Payton?" he whispered into the phone.

"Hello, John."

The detective couldn't believe his ears. His sister's voice was coming through loud and clear, and she sounded happy. Maybe even ecstatic.

"Are you all right?" he asked in amazement.

"I'm fine," she answered giddily. "Why wouldn't I be?"

John shuddered as an unholy mess of emotions coursed through him—relief, shame, grief—and then stared at his cell phone in disbelief. It was clear his sister had no clue what she'd just put him through. He'd been on the rollercoaster from hell while she'd been who knew where. He decided to cut directly to the chase.

"Where the hell have you—"

A shooting pain in his right shoulder interrupted the conversation, and the accompanying jolt sent his cell phone flying.

He hit the floor and rolled with the blow, looking up just in time to see Vladimir standing over him, blood dripping from his fingernails.

John reached for his shoulder. The magician had sliced through his shirt and left a neat row of lacerations. "Goddamn!" he said and stared in shock at the blood on his hand. *His* blood.

"John?"

He turned to see his cell phone laying on the floor, the speaker phone apparently having been activated as it skidded across the black-and-gray-tiled floor.

"John!" his sister repeated frantically, her voice sounding tinny. "What's going on?"

Before he could respond, Vladimir lunged at him, pulling him up by his T-shirt until their eyes were only inches apart. The magician's face, twisted in violence, bulging with excitement, hardly looked recognizable, but the longer John stared into his eyes, the more he understood he wasn't looking at hate or even lust, just pure, wild fear.

"I am going to give you what you wanted to give me," Vladimir said, his voice trembling. And with his right hand, he yanked a nearby easel free from the painting it had been supporting. As the framed artwork fell to the floor, its glass shattering, he hurriedly went to work on one of the easel's legs, finally prying most of it loose and producing a jagged point in the process. "There," he said and brandished the weapon at the detective. "Medicine for the self-righteous."

"Self-righteous?" a woman asked.

John wriggled free from Vladimir's grip and scrambled to his feet.

Both men squinted as the lights in the hallway went from dim to brilliant in a flash.

"If he's self-righteous," Sadie said, moving pantherlike from the bank of light switches to Vladimir, "you're the fucking pope." She kicked the improvised stake from his right hand and smiled brazenly.

"You!" Vladimir hissed.

"Me!" she squealed, mocking the magician. She was dressed to kill in a vinyl cat suit and holding a sawed-off shotgun.

John hurried to his phone, which was still chirping with Payton's frantic pleas, and picked it up off the floor. "I'm okay," he reassured his sister, clicking off the speaker phone as he spoke. "Can you hold on a second?"

"Okay," she said in worried tone.

Vladimir was still sneering at Sadie. "You whore! You gave the video to that reporter woman!"

"Guilty," Sadie said and nodded to John without taking her eyes off Vladimir. "A word of advice, detective. Next time you meet up with a vampire, shoot first and ask questions later. Vladdy here can't resist a little showmanship. So all you have to do is blow him into itty-bitty pieces while he's dreaming up his next line."

Vladimir raised his hand in protest, and Sadie pulled the trigger, tearing his hand free and part of his face with it. Before he could recover from the blast, she pulled the trigger again, this time blasting a whole in his gut the size of a Frisbee. Again, the magician lurched and then lifted his other hand in protest, another speech on his lips, but Sadie pumped two more rounds into him, and he fell to his knees and then onto his back, gasping for breath in agony.

"While the vampire is trying to put himself back together," she said and knelt beside him, "finish him." And businesslike, she removed the beautiful wooden cross that had been dangling above her breasts, and with superhuman strength, she rammed the pointed end through Vladimir's heart.

The magician disappeared into dust before he could make a sound.

John opened his mouth to say something but stopped after the first word. "You—"

Sadie stood up and turned to face the detective, a smirk on her lips and the devil in her eyes. "Hello, cowboy."

"You," John continued to stammer, "you killed him."

Sadie delivered another devastating pout. "I'm sorry. Shall I resuscitate him?"

"No," John said.

Sadie gestured to the cell phone still in John's hands.

"She's okay then?"

"I guess so," he said. "Do you mind if I—"

"Take your time."

John turned his back to Sadie and retreated a few steps. "Hey, kid."

"John! What's going on?"

"It's nothing," he said. "Someone was just trying to kill me. Business as usual."

"What?"

"It's okay. Problem solved." He still couldn't believe he was talking to his sister, but the relief in hearing her voice was short-lived, tainted end to end as it was in resentment, frustration, guilt, an ugly potpourri of emotions that needed venting. "So," he said, remembering the question he'd begun moments earlier before Vladimir had attacked him, "where the hell have you been?"

"What do you mean?" Payton replied defensively. "I left you a message. You did get my message, didn't you?"

"Yes, but you didn't say you were going to *disappear* for Christ's sake. You haven't been answering your cell phone or anything."

"Sorry," she said meekly. "They don't have service on the island, except at the airport. I'm flying back tonight."

"*Island?*"

"Yes!" Payton squealed. "I've been in the Bahamas doing a photo shoot—and you won't believe for who."

"For *whom*. I thought you were a schoolteacher."

"Listen to you, big brother. Gosh. You'd think you'd just be happy I'm going to be on the cover of the next issue of *Glamour*."

John didn't know whether to laugh or cry. He turned long enough to see Sadie fidgeting a few feet away, deadly cross still in hand. "Look, kid, I gotta go."

"Will you call me tomorrow?"

"Sure," he said and hung up. He turned to face the woman to whom he owed his life. "Thanks," he said. "You saved my ass."

"And now," Sadie said, drawing closer, "you're going to save mine."

She handed him the sharp-ended cross she'd just used on Vladimir. "Do me like you mean it."

John felt himself backing up. "No. No, I can't—"

She closed the gap between them and hurriedly pressed her lips against his, but unlike their last embrace, this one was pure tenderness, their eyes wide open.

"You know what I think?" she whispered.

"No," he said, wishing he could lose himself in her hazel eyes forever.

"I think you can."

CHAPTER 18

IT HADN'T BEEN a perfect conspiracy. Just a perfect clusterfuck.

As it turned out, Vladimir hadn't been an evil mastermind, just a magnificent, if somewhat self-absorbed and amoral, entertainer trying to make a living, one who happened to be a vampire. He had operated on the rather simple but cutthroat principle that the show must go on. Toward that end, he had blackmailed the mayor, killed anybody who tried to follow the trail of dead bodies that began and ended at Dracula's Castle, and manipulated those in his inner circle to do his bidding, all the while perfecting his act. In the end, his dedication to the show had ultimately proved his undoing. He thought like an artist, not like a criminal.

Alistair Bishop? John was pretty sure Angela had been right about him. The guy liked to wear his pajamas to parties, but that didn't make him evil, just eccentric and a bad dresser. He was harmless, although the same couldn't be said for his dark imagination, which had come to life in Dracula's Castle.

Chief Lowman? Detective Pettit? Cronies, yes. Assholes, definitely. They were willing to do whatever was necessary to hold on to their jobs and their respective positions in the department pecking order, but John's guess was they had been taking orders from a certain compromised politician. The mayor had told them to look the other way when it came to Dracula's Castle, and they'd done exactly that. Hear no evil, see no evil. Vegas would be better off without men like them on the payroll, obviously. However, John wasn't going to cast stones at the LVPD. The police back in New Orleans had a reputation at least as ugly, and loose canons like him didn't exactly own the moral high ground. Thanks to a certain beautiful vampire, he knew exactly who he was and what he was meant to do.

Apollo? T-Bone? A couple of cogs in the machine. Evil didn't happen without somebody willing to goose-step along for the ride.

As for the hapless mayor, well, he wasn't so hapless. He'd done himself and the citizens of Las Vegas a huge disservice by living a lie. Maybe he could have been an accomplished painter. A loving mother. Instead, he was drowning in corruption and doing everything he could to keep his skeletons in the closet, even if that meant sacrificing the lives of others. For him, a reckoning was in order, but John wouldn't be the one to deliver it. He'd leave that to the state attorney's office.

John took another sip of straight black coffee in the elevator and watched the numbers light up one after the other until he reached the top floor. Once in the lobby, he tossed his cup of coffee into a garbage can and then proceeded to walk straight past the receptionist.

"Excuse me!" she hollered after him. "You can't go in there! The mayor is in a meeting!"

John pushed the door open and found the mayor alone in his office, staring at a computer.

The mayor looked up at John, a blank expression on his face. "You don't look like an attorney ... or a bureaucrat. Reporter?"

"Keep guessing," John said and eased himself into a chair opposite the mayor.

The receptionist appeared in the doorway. "I'm sorry, Mr. Mayor. I don't know who this gentleman is. He ... got past me."

John tossed the videotape Vladimir had been using to blackmail him onto the mayor's desk.

Mayor Ward studied it briefly and then glanced up at his receptionist with a strained look on his face. "It's all right, Sissy. You can leave us."

The receptionist frowned, lingering in the doorway just long enough to give John a disapproving glance, and then disappeared.

"Do you know what this is?" John asked and motioned to the tape.

"I think so, yes. You must be Sadie's detective friend."

"She told you about me?"

The mayor nodded nonchalantly. "We talk all the time. She's a beautiful soul."

"What did you talk about yesterday when you met her in the parking garage outside Bloodgood Booking?"

The mayor's face flushed red. "She arranged the meeting. Said she had some bad news." He stared at the tape quietly a moment. "She said she'd dropped this off with a reporter—she called it the 'anonymous tip of a lifetime'—and told me all hell was about to break loose. Said this was my chance to get out while the getting was good. Or stay and face up to my past."

John cocked his head in confusion. "I don't get it. If you were such good friends with Sadie, why was she torturing you in front of a video camera? And why'd she give the tape to Angela Ramirez?"

"To answer your first question, people can change, even if nine times out of ten they fail. The first time I ever saw Sadie was that night you saw on the videotape. I had been to a few of Vladimir's parties, had too much to drink at one of them. What can I say? Loose lips sink ships, right? Vladimir must have been worried about the attention the casino was getting from the missing girls' case, so he arranged for a little dinner party, drugged my wine, and voilà—caught me on tape incriminating myself. Anyway, I could tell Sadie's heart wasn't in it, even when she was doing her best to humiliate me. She started dropping in on me from time to time after that. At first, I thought it was to keep me intimidated, but eventually, I realized she felt bad about the whole thing and was looking for a way to atone for everything. We started talking. Turned out we had a lot in common. Both of us were uncomfortable in our own skin. She had had big plans before she had met Vladimir, you know. She was gonna be a star—and without compromising her values. She had an excellent work ethic. And what beauty!

"As far as your second question is concerned, as much as Sadie cares for me, she absolutely despises Vladimir. When she first met him, she was an impressionable young woman with the future ahead of her. By the time he was through with her, she was dead inside. I think the only thing that keeps her going these days is the idea of burying that monster. Then again, when she talks about you, I swear I see a little spark in her eyes."

John closed his eyes and tried to let his memory go blank. The last thing he wanted to remember was Sadie's beautiful gaze. He looked up at the mayor. "So you've decided to stay and face up to your past."

"I have. It's going to be painful. And embarrassing. And the end of my political career, I'm sure. But just the same—" The mayor took the tape and dropped it into his bottom desk drawer. "No one needs to see this." He chuckled resignedly. "Thank you, detective. You could have kept it, you know, to hold my feet to the fire."

"I've got no beef with your private life, Mr. Mayor, and I'm sure the state attorney will be addressing your *public* one in fine detail."

The mayor shook his head. "It's all over now anyway. I've

already been indicted. I'm ready to do penance. What about you, detective? You look like someone with a heavy heart."

John stood up and shook the mayor's hand. "You have no idea," he said and excused himself.

Vladimir. Alistair Bishop. Chief Lowman and Detective Pettit. Apollo. T-Bone. The mayor. So much for the lengthy list of people John planned to forget.

As for the short list, he couldn't bear to repeat her name—and doubted he'd be able to anytime soon.

He stepped into the elevator and watched as the doors closed and the mayor's receptionist disappeared from view. The elevator lurched downward, and he keyed his cell phone.

As numb as he felt inside, he knew he couldn't hold Payton responsible for the way things had turned out. Others had already paid the ultimate price for his mad rush to save a sister who didn't need saving. All that was left to do was to welcome Payton back to civilization. She was alive and well—a considerable accomplishment considering how close she'd come to joining Vladimir's show.

"Hello?" Payton answered on the third ring.

"Hey, kid."

"John! Boy, am I glad to hear your voice! What happened last night?"

"Long story," he said. "What do you say I take you out for dinner?"

"When? Are you coming to Vegas sometime soon?"

"How 'bout I pick you up at six o'clock?"

His sister shrieked like a teenage girl. "What? Tonight? You're here now?"

"That's right, kid, and I wanna hear all about the Bahamas."

"Oh, my God, it was incredible!" she said, clearly eager to recap her adventure. "I was living life first class all the way. But John, you won't believe what happened while I was gone. Here I am on sabbatical, trying like crazy to forget about teaching, and last night when I get home, I go through all my voice mails—you sure sounded worried, brother—and one of 'em is from a friend back in the Bronx telling me my students voted me teacher of the year!"

"That's beautiful."

"I know." His sister paused long enough to breathe. "John?"

"Yeah?"

"You sound tired."

"It's been a busy couple of weeks."

"Why? What have you been up to?"

"We can talk about it at dinner."

"Let me guess—a long story."

"Right."

~~~

For the first time in weeks, the skies opened up over Las Vegas. The scorched earth, everywhere an open wound of fissures and clefts several inches deep, looked too brittle to accept the gift.

John paused outside the passenger's side of his recently cleaned rental car and inhaled deeply the smell of fresh rain on dry blacktop, and as he lingered over the scent, he realized, suddenly at first, then with a longing almost too painful to indulge, how much he missed New Orleans. The place was rotting and neglected and falling apart at the seams, but it was home, nonetheless: lush, overgrown, and ripe for change. Maybe it would never live up to its potential. But hope was enough, at least for now, and it was more than Vegas, a city built on calculated fantasy, would ever give anyone.

"Why don't you just kill me now?" Sadie said as she emerged from the VW, squinting up at the rain.

She was a stunning apparition, too beautiful to be real, in a knee-length, backless black dress. She was graceful, sophisticated, the very embodiment of feminine beauty.

John took her slender hand in his while he offered the

protection of an oversized umbrella. "Maybe later," he said, smiling at the sight of the gorgeous vampire cringing in the rain. "Come on. There's someone I'd like you to meet."

The two walked slowly in the rain from the cemetery's circular drive to a rolling patch of lawn, framed perfectly by a pair of Italian cypresses, where a modest gathering of people, all dressed in dark hues, had gathered somberly around a freshly excavated hole in the ground.

Chief Lowman stood in front along with Detective Pettit, each of them assuming the stoic countenance of someone who had lost a comrade in arms. They were here to bury Officer Harry "Pudge" Feineman, but they would soon forget him and the sacrifice he'd made before his coffin even hit the dirt, for to acknowledge his death would be to face their own failures as officers of the law and as supposed men of decency.

John guided Sadie, her hand still cradled in his, until they'd found a place to stand slightly off to the side and behind the others.

"Who are we burying?" Sadie whispered.

"Someone I have a hunch you knew," John whispered back.

She frowned, eyeing him suspiciously.

A graying Catholic priest dressed in a black suit and white collar and braving the elements without an umbrella began the ceremonies with a reading.

"From the Psalm of David," he said, just loud enough to be heard, "*The Lord is my shepherd. I shall not want. He maketh me to lie down in green pastures. He leadeth me beside the still waters. He restoreth my soul. He leadeth me in the path of righteousness for his name's sake.*"

John glanced at Sadie and could see her fidgeting beneath the umbrella. What was the difference between her and her heartless mentor? Vladimir had killed without remorse. So had she. Of that, John was certain. Vladimir had lived like a high-class parasite, traveling in posh circles while dining on the blood of mostly beautiful women, mostly new to Vegas, mostly without local ties of any kind. His had been a deliberate and carefully orchestrated lifestyle, one aimed solely at propping up his career. Blood for fame. Sadie? She had learned from the best, but she was still wild. Unpredictable. Combustible. Vladimir had stolen what had made her human, but he hadn't conquered her soul. Could she get it back? Did she deserve the chance?

"Yea, though I walk through the valley of the shadow of Death, I shall fear no evil. For thou art with me; thy rod and thy staff, they comfort me."

As John studied the beautiful woman at his side, he remembered another girl, nearly as intoxicating, and felt a shiver run through him. Sadie wasn't the only one in search of atonement. He needed it, too.

"Thou preparest a table before me in the presence of mine enemies. Thou anointest my head with oil; my cup runneth over. Surely goodness and mercy shall follow me all the days of my life, and I will dwell in the house of the Lord forever."

The priest looked up at the assembly of policemen, family, and friends, and for the first time, he named the deceased. "We are gathered here today to honor the life and deeds of Officer Harry S. Feineman, a dedicated professional who gave his life in the service of his fellow man."

A look of recognition slowly spread across Sadie's face, and her eyes widened in disbelief and then just as quickly narrowed. "You bastard!" she hissed at John. "Get me the fuck out of here!"

Instead of letting her go, John pulled her closer. "I won't let you out of this one, even if you make a scene." He leveled his gaze to hers and was momentarily taken aback by the fear in her eyes.

"Are you doing this just to make me suffer?" she asked, her lips trembling.

"No," he whispered in reply. It was hard to make his case

with a graveside service going on only a few feet away. "I want you to live," John said. He had begun the sentence with more in mind but realized this was as good a place to stop as any. He couldn't put into words exactly what he felt.

A bundle of white, hot fury only seconds earlier, Sadie buried her head in his shoulder. Maybe she knew better than he did about what he was trying to say.

The service went on for another twenty minutes—too long in Detective O'Meara's estimation. But it ended the right way with a twenty-one gun salute.

The rain, which had poured throughout, finally let up as the crowd dispersed.

Judy Feineman had just said good-bye to an older gentleman, one of the last to leave, when John caught her gaze.

"Detective O'Meara!" she said and waved for him to come to him.

He did as she asked, dragging Sadie with him.

"I'm glad you were able to make it."

"It was the least I could do," John replied and offered a consoling hug.

"I was a good girl," Judy said with a gleam in her eyes. "Just like I promised I'd be."

"That you were. I figured you'd try to put Chief Lowman in a headlock or something."

She laughed, her chubby cheeks growing rosy, and then dabbed at her bloodshot eyes with a tissue. "It was tempting, but I figured Harry wouldn't approve. He was always such a perfect gentleman." She turned her attention to Sadie, whose hand John still held firmly in his. "Detective, please tell me you found your sister."

"I did," John said. "She's safe and sound."

"Is this—?" Judy began.

"No," John answered quickly. "This is Sadie, a friend of mine."

"Oh," Judy said. "I didn't think she was your sister. You two seem more like ... well, what I mean to say is ... you're obviously very much in—"

John raised his hand to stop her, but Sadie elbowed him in the side.

"Let her finish," Sadie said.

"No, no," Judy said, "you don't want me to finish. I'm so addled right now I don't know my right from left." Her eyes welled up. "Did you know my Harry?"

Sadie glanced away nervously, the shoe suddenly on the other foot, and John could feel her hand grow clammy in his.

"I—"

"Never mind, honey," Judy said. "I'm just glad you came. You're a beautiful sight, and I'm sure it would have meant a great deal to Harry to have you here."

"This might not be the place," John said, changing gears slightly, "but I wanted to be the first to tell you that the man responsible for your husband's death is no longer among the living."

Judy's face, sweet and full of color only moments earlier, paled suddenly, and an icy stare replaced her smile. She looked up at the sky and then returned her gaze to John. "Thank you, detective. Thank you."

~~~

"What now?" Sadie asked.

She was staring at him, her arms folded, her back against the car door, as she waited for an answer.

He remembered the sycamores in his dream, the feeling that he could drown in her and not regret a thing.

"I'm going home," he said.

"Just like that?"

"Just like that."

"So why spare me? Why drag me to this goddamned cemetery so I could watch Judy cry?"

"You remembered her name."

"Of course."

"That's a start."

Sadie slowly shook her head in anger. "I understand what you're trying to do, detective. I do. But look at me," she said, her hands trembling visibly. "I'm a mess." She took his hands in hers. "Do you feel that? I haven't eaten in two days. I haven't slept. I haven't done anything except—"

"You're not a monster."

"No? Then why do I look at people and see dinner? Why do I wanna kiss you one minute and kill you the next?"

John laughed. "Hey, I'm not a vampire, and I feel the same way about you."

"You just said a mouthful. You're not a vampire. Vladimir's dead, and the mayor's toast. And you get to walk away from here and forget about all of us."

"Except you."

"Why are you doing this to me?"

"Because I believe in you."

She pushed him away. "Don't you get it, detective? Vampires don't do happiness! Vampires don't get happy endings! It's eat or be eaten. That's it. That's all we have."

"Maybe," John said. "But you're not like the rest of them. You're different."

She groaned in frustration. "I give up. You're hopeless."

"You're right about that," John said and walked to the other side of the car to get in. "So are you coming or not?"

Sadie turned to face him, only her face and the top of her shoulders visible above the VW's roof. Her hazel eyes pleaded with his, but she was obviously afraid to say what was in her heart. It was the same vulnerable look that had bewitched him from the beginning. "You'll drop me off at my place?"

"Sure. I'm taking my sister out to dinner before I leave. That should give you a couple hours to go back to your place and pack your things."

Her beautiful eyes narrowed. "Pack? For what?"

John ignored the question and ducked inside.

Sadie opened her side and leaned over but stopped there.

"Get in," he said and motioned for her to climb inside.

She refused, still squinting at him suspiciously. "What am I packing for, detective?"

It was a good question, and one John wasn't sure he could answer to anyone's satisfaction, least of all his. He couldn't bring Jenny back. Couldn't undo the mess he'd made. But he had come too far, risked too much, not to bet the house on Sadie. Maybe she was a vampire, but she wasn't hopeless, her own pessimism notwithstanding. Like everybody else, she deserved a second chance, something Jenny had won and then lost just as quickly, thanks in both cases to his impulsiveness. Had it not been for him, Jenny would have never made it out of the Lower Nine—only to die twice.

"Your new life," he finally answered. "And bring a windbreaker. Hurricane season's coming."

EPILOGUE

Eugene Bettencourt opened the door to his office and turned on the light.

"Another day, another dollar," he mumbled to himself as he shuffled inside and closed the door behind him.

He took off his cap, hung it on a peg behind the door, and then set his thermos down on his desk. He normally didn't get started this early in the morning, but showbiz was funny that way. Routine was nice but rarely enjoyed. Business hours were handy but rarely observed. The show went on, and with it, all the behind-the-scenes work that made the magic come to life was done.

He sat down behind his desk, dialed a long distance number, and waited. Transatlantic calls weren't unheard of, but they were rare enough to take pleasure in. Even the ring tones sounded exotic.

"*Bună Ziua*," a woman answered after the third chime.

"*Bună Ziua*," Eugene said, returning the Romanian greeting. "I need to speak with your boss."

He leaned back in his chair and waited. Showbiz was all about connections, and nobody was better connected than Eugene Bettencourt.

Finally, a man answered gruffly, "What is it?"

"Sorry to bother you, old friend," Eugene said, "but I'm short an illusionist. I need you to send me another one ASAP. The show must go on."

About the Author

Timothy Gray is a lifelong resident of Illinois who successfully practices orthopedic surgery in Effingham. He was born and raised in the small town of Cullom, Illinois, which had a population of six hundred. He had earned degrees from the University of Illinois in Champaign-Urbana as well as Chicago for medical school and residency. (He bleeds orange and blue). He married his high school sweetheart, and he has four lovely children, who currently range from twenty-two to sixteen years of age. His life is currently consumed by college visits, high school sporting events, and a busy orthopedic practice. Along with these activities, he has always had a passion for the written word and has always dreamed of seeing his words in print. In the past, he has made several attempts to generate a novel, but *The Magician* is the first that he has been able to bring to completion with satisfactory dialogue and plot development. He is currently working on the sequel to this book, *Bad Vodoo*.